Midnight

By Octavus Roy Cohen

Originally published in 1921

Midnight

Published by Intrepid Ink, LLC

Intrepid Ink, LLC provides full publishing services to
authors of fiction and non-fiction books, eBooks and
websites. From editing to formatting, to publishing, to
marketing, Intrepid Ink gets your creative works into the
hands of the people who want to read them.
Find out more at www.IntrepidInk.com.

ISBN 13: 978-1-935774-10-5

Printed in the United States of America

FOREWORD

Midnight, by Octavus Roy Cohen, is interesting not only for its story, but also because it marks a transition in American detective fiction. Most earlier American mysteries had followed the British tradition of the gentleman amateur detective solving crimes of the upper classes, mostly involving money or passion. With *Midnight*, Cohen takes a step towards the noir fiction of the thirties and forties. His detective, David Carroll, while a gentleman, is working from inside the police department, the parties involved are middle class at best, and the motives in the crime are definitely on the sordid side, worthy of Dashiell Hammett or Raymond Chandler.

To be sure, David Carroll, the detective in the story, is anything but "hard-boiled." He is young, fresh-faced, and much more comfortable using his intellect than a gun. But in the end, the mystery is solved not with a brilliant flash of deductive logic, but with "leg-work," the patient tracking down of leads until everything falls in place.

Cohen may have been ahead of his time with *Midnight* but that didn't keep him from providing a first rate mystery.

About the Author

Octavus Roy Cohen (1891-1959) was born in South Carolina. After working as a newspaper man he was admitted to the South Carolina bar in 1913. He published 56 books including both detective and humorous fiction. Many of his stories appeared in *The Saturday Evening Post*. He also wrote plays and radio and film scripts. Several of his books were made into movies including "Curtain at Eight" based on his novel *The Backstage Mystery*.

Greg Fowlkes
Editor-In-Chief
Resurrected Press
www.ResurrectedPress.com

TO DR. MILES A. WATKINS

TABLE OF CONTENTS

1
OUT OF THE STORM

Taxicab No. 92,381 skidded crazily on the icy pavement of Atlantic Avenue. Spike Walters, its driver, cursed roundly as he applied the brakes and with difficulty obtained control of the little closed car. Depressing the clutch pedal, he negotiated the frozen thoroughfare and parked his car in the lee of the enormous Union Station, which bulked forbiddingly in the December midnight.

Atlantic Avenue was deserted. The lights at the main entrance of the Union Station glowed frigidly. Opposite, a single arc-lamp on the corner of Cypress Street cast a white, cheerless light on the gelid pavement. The few stores along the avenue were dark, with the exception of the warmly lighted White Star restaurant directly opposite the Stygian spot where Spike's car was parked.

The city was in the grip of the first cold wave of the year. For two days the rain had fallen—a nasty, drizzling rain which made the going soggy and caused people to greet one another with frowns. Late that afternoon the mercury had started a rapid downward journey. Fires were piled high in the furnaces, automobile-owners poured alcohol into their radiators. The streets were deserted early, and the citizens, for the most part, had retired shiveringly under mountains of blankets and down quilts still redolent of moth-balls.

Winter had come with freezing blasts which swept around corners and chilled to the bone. The rain of two days became a driving sleet, which formed a mirror of ice over the city.

On the seat of his yellow taxicab, Spike Walters drew a heavy lap-robe more closely about his husky figure and shivered miserably. Fortunately, the huge bulk of the station to his right protected him in a large measure from the shrieking wintry winds. Mechanically Spike kept his eyes focused upon the station entrance, half a block ahead.

But no one was there. Nowhere was there a sign of life, nowhere an indication of warmth or cheer or comfort. With fingers so numb that they were almost powerless to do the bidding of his mind, Spike drew forth his watch and glanced at it. Midnight!

Spike replaced the watch, blew on his numb fingers in a futile effort to restore warmth, slipped his hands back into a pair of heavy–but, on this night, entirely inadequate–driving-gloves, and gave himself over to a mental rebellion against the career of a professional taxi-driver.

"Worst night I've ever known," he growled to himself; and he was not far wrong.

Midnight! No train due until 12.25, and that an accommodation from some small town up-State. No taxi fares on such a train as that. The north-bound fast train–headed for New York–that was late, too. Due at 11.55, Spike had seen a half-frozen station-master mark it up as being fifty minutes late. Perhaps a passenger to be picked up there–some sleepy, disgruntled, entirely unhappy person eager to attain the warmth and coziness of a big hotel.

Yet Spike knew that he must wait. The company for which he worked specialized on service. It boasted that every train was met by a yellow taxicab–and this was Spike's turn for all-night duty at the Union Station.

All the independent taxi-drivers had long since deserted their posts. The parking space on Cypress Street, opposite the main entrance of the station–a space usually crowded with commercial cars–was deserted. No private cars were there, either. Spike seemed alone in the drear December night, his car an exotic of the early winter.

Ten minutes passed—fifteen. The cold bit through Spike's overcoat, battled to the skin, and chewed to the bone. It was well nigh unbearable. The young taxi-driver's lips became blue. He tried to light a cigarette, but his fingers were unable to hold the match.

He looked around. A street-car, bound for a suburb, passed noisily. It paused briefly before the railroad-station, neither discharging nor taking on a passenger, then clanged protestingly on its way. Impressed in Spike's mind was a mental picture of the chilled motorman, and of the conductor huddled over the electric heater within the car. Spike felt a personal resentment against that conductor. Comfort seemed unfair on a night like this; heat a luxury more to be desired than much fine gold.

From across the street the light of the White Star Cafe beckoned. Ordinarily Spike was not a patron of the White Star, nor other eating establishments of its class. The White Star was notoriously unsanitary, its food poisonously indigestible; but as Spike's eyes were held hypnotically by the light he thought of two things—within the circle of that light he could find heat and a scalding liquid which was flavored with coffee.

The vision was too much for Spike. The fast train, due now at 12.45, might bring a fare. It was well beyond the bounds of reason that he would get a passenger from the accommodation due in a few minutes. There were no casuals abroad.

The young driver clambered with difficulty from his seat. He staggered as he tried to stand erect, his numb limbs protesting against the burden of his healthy young body. A gale howled around the dark Jackson Street corner of the long, rambling station, and Spike defensively covered both ears with his gloved hands.

He made his way eagerly across the street; slipping and sliding on the glassy surface, head bent against the driving sleet, clothes crackling where particles of ice had formed. Spike reached the door of the eating-house, opened it, and almost staggered as the warmth of the place smote him like a hot blast.

For a few seconds he stood motionless, reveling in the sheer animal comfort of the change. Then he made his way to the counter, seated himself on a revolving stool, and looked up at the waiter who came stolidly forward from the big, round-bellied stove at the rear.

"Hello, George!"

The restaurateur nodded.

"Hello!"

"My gosh! What a night!"

"Pretty cold, ain't it?"

"Cold?" Spike Walters looked up antagonistically. "Say, you don't know what cold means. I'd rather have your job to-night than a million dollars. Only if I had a million dollars I'd buy twenty stoves, set 'em in a circle, build a big fire in each one, sit in the middle, and tell winter to go to thunder–that's what I'd do. Now, George, hustle and lay me out a cup of coffee, hot–get that?–and a couple of them greasy doughnuts of yourn."

The coffee and doughnuts were duly produced, and the stolid Athenian retired to the torrid zone of his stove. Spike bravely tried one of the doughnuts and gave it up as a bad job, but he quaffed the coffee with an eagerness which burned his throat and imparted a pleasing sensation of inward warmth. Then he stretched luxuriously and lighted a cigarette.

He glanced through the long-unwashed window of the White Star Cafe–"Ladies and gents welcome," it announced–and shuddered at the prospect of again braving the elements. Across the street his unprotesting taxicab stood parked parallel to the curb; beyond it glowered the end of the station. To the right of the long, rambling structure he could see the occasional glare of switch engines and track-walkers' lanterns in the railroad yards.

As he looked, he saw the headlight of the locomotive at the head of the accommodation split the gloom. Instinctively Spike rose, paid his check, and stood uncomfortably at the door, buttoning the coat tightly around his neck.

Of course it was impossible that the accommodation carried a fare for him; but then duty was duty, and Spike took exceeding pride in the company for which he worked. The company's slogan of service was part of Spike's creed. He opened the door, recoiled for a second as the gale swept angrily against him, then plunged blindly across the street. He clambered into the seat of his cab, depressed the starter, and eventually was answered by the reluctant cough of the motor. He raced it for a while, getting the machinery heated up preparatory to the possibility of a run.

Then he saw the big doors at the main entrance of the station open and a few melancholy passengers, brought to town by the accommodation train, step to the curb, glance about in search of a street-car, and then duck back into the station. Spike shoved his clutch in and crawled forward along the curb, leaving the inky shadows of the far end of the station, and emerging finally into the effulgence of the arc at the corner of Cypress Street.

Once again the door of the Union Station opened. This time Spike took a professional interest in the person who stepped uncertainly out into the night. Long experience informed him that this was a fare.

She was of medium height, and comfortably guarded against the frigidity of the night by a long fur coat buttoned snugly around her neck. She wore a small squirrel tam, and was heavily veiled. In her right hand she carried a large suit-case and in her left a purse.

She stepped to the curb and looked around inquiringly. She signalled the cab. Even as he speeded his car forward, Spike wondered at her indifference to the almost unbearable cold.

"Cab, miss?"

He pulled up short before her.

"Yes." Her tone was almost curt. She had her hand on the door handle before Spike could make a move to alight. "Drive to 981 East End Avenue."

Without leaving the driver's seat, Spike reached for her suit-case and put it beside him. The woman–a young woman, Spike reflected–stepped inside and slammed the door. Spike fed the gas and started, whirling south on Atlantic Avenue for two blocks, and then turning to his left across the long viaduct which marks the beginning of East End Avenue.

He settled himself for a long and unpleasant drive. To reach 981 East End Avenue he had to drive nearly five miles straight in the face of the December gale.

And then he found himself wondering about the woman. Her coat–a rich fur thing of black and gray–her handbag, her whole demeanor–all bespoke affluence. She had probably been visiting at some little town, and had come down on the accommodation; but no one had been there to meet her. Anyway, Spike found himself too miserable and too cold to reflect much about his passenger.

He drove into a head wind. The sleet slapped viciously against his windshield and stuck there. The patent device he carried for the purpose of clearing rain away refused to work. Spike shoved his windshield up in order to afford a vision of the icy asphalt ahead.

And then he grew cold in earnest. He seemed to freeze all the way through. He drove mechanically, becoming almost numb as the wind, unimpeded now, struck him squarely. He lost all interest in what he was doing or where he was going. He called himself a fool for having left the cozy warmth of the White Star Cafe. He told himself–

Suddenly he clamped on the brakes. It was a narrow squeak! The end of the long freight train rumbled on into the night. Spike hadn't seen it; only the racket of the big cars as they crossed East End Avenue, and then the lights on the rear of the caboose, had warned him.

He stopped his car for perhaps fifteen seconds to make sure that the crossing was clear, then started on again, a bit shaken by the narrow escape. He bumped cautiously across the railroad tracks.

The rest of the journey was a nightmare. The suburb through which he was passing seemed to have congealed. Save for the corner lights, there was no sign of life. The roofs and sidewalks glistened with ice. Occasionally the car struck a bump and skidded dangerously. Spike had forgotten his passenger, forgotten the restaurant, the coffee, the weather itself. He only remembered that he was cold–almost unbearably cold.

Then he began taking note of the houses. There was No. 916. He looked ahead. These were houses of the poorer type, the homes of laborers situated on the outer edge of the suburb of East End. Funny–the handsomely dressed woman–such a poor neighborhood–

He came to a halt before a dilapidated bungalow which squatted darkly in the night. Stiff with cold, he reached his hand back to the door on the right of the car, and with difficulty opened it. Then he spoke:

"Here y'are, miss–No. 981!"

There was no answer. Spike repeated:

"Here y'are, miss."

Still no answer. Spike clambered stiffly from the car, circled to the curb, and stuck his head in the door.

"Here, miss–"

Spike stepped back. Then he again put his head inside the cab.

"Well, I'll be–"

The thing was impossible, and yet it was true. Spike gazed at the seat. The woman had disappeared!

The thing was absurd; impossible. He had seen her get into the cab at the Union Station. There, in the front of the car, was her suit-case; but she had gone—disappeared completely, vanished without leaving a sign. Momentarily forgetful of the cold, Spike found a match and lighted it. Holding it cupped in his hands, he peered within the cab. Then he recoiled with a cry of horror.

For, huddled on the floor, he discerned the body of a man!

2
THE SUIT-CASE IS OPENED

The barren trees which lined the broad deserted thoroughfare jutted starkly into the night, waving their menacing, ice-crusted arms. The December gale, sweeping westward, shrieked through the glistening branches. It shrieked warning and horror, howled and sighed, sighed and howled.

Spike Walters felt suddenly ill. He forgot the cold, and was conscious of a fear which acted like a temporary anesthesia. For a few seconds he stood staring, until the match which he held burned out and scorched the flesh of his fingers. His jaw dropped, his eyes widened. He opened his lips and tried to speak, but closed them again without having uttered a sound save a choking gasp. He tried again, feeling an urge for speech—something, anything, to make him believe that he was here, alive—that the horror within the cab was real. This time he uttered an "Oh, my God!"

The words seemed to vitalize him. He fumbled for another match, found it, and lighted it within the cab. It seemed to have the radiance of an incandescent.

Spike had hoped that his first impression would prove to be a mere figment of his imagination; but now there was no doubting. There, sprawled in an ugly, inhuman heap on the floor, head resting against the cushioned seat of the cab, was the figure of a man. There was no doubt that he was dead. Even Spike, young, optimistic, and unversed in the ways of death as he was, knew that he was alone with a corpse.

And as he gazed, a strange courage came to him. He found himself emboldened to investigate. He was shivering while he did so, shivering with fear and with the terrific cold of the night. He could not quite bring himself to touch the body, but he did not need to move it to see that murder had been done.

The clothes told him instantly that the man was of high social station. They were obviously expensive clothes, probably tailor-made. The big coat, open at the top, was flung back. Beneath, Spike discerned a gray tweed—and on the breast of the gray tweed was a splotch, a dark, ugly thing which appeared black and was not black. Spike shuddered. He had never liked the sight of blood.

The match spluttered and went out. Spike looked around. He felt hopelessly alone. Not a pedestrian; not a light. The houses, set well back from the street, were dark, forbiddingly dark.

He saw a street-car rattle past, bound on the final run of the night for the car-sheds at East End. Then he was alone again—alone and frightened.

He felt the necessity for action. He must do something—something, but what? What was there to do?

A great fear gripped him. He was with the body. The body was in his cab. He would be arrested for the murder of the man!

Of course he knew he didn't do it. The woman had committed the murder.

Spike swore. He had almost forgotten the woman. Where was she? How had she managed to leave the taxicab? When had the man, who now lay sprawled in the cab, entered it?

He had driven straight from the Union Station to the address given by the woman—straight down East End Avenue, turning neither to right nor left. The utter impossibilty of the situation robbed it of some of its stark horror. And yet—

Spike knew that he must do something. He tried to think connectedly, and found it a difficult task. Near him loomed the shadow which was No. 981 East End Avenue—

the address given by the woman when she entered the cab.

He might go in there and report the circumstances. Someone there would know who she was, and—but he hesitated.

Perhaps this thing had been prearranged. Perhaps they would get him—for what he didn't know. When a man—a young man—comes face to face with murder for the first time, making its acquaintance on a freezing December midnight and in a lonely spot, he is not to be blamed if his mental equilibrium is destroyed.

Wild plans chased each other through his brain. He might dump the body by the roadside and run back to town. That was absurd on the face of it, for he would be convicting himself when the body was found. It would be traced to him in some way—he knew that. He was already determined to keep away from No. 981 East End Avenue. There was something sinister in the unfriendly shadow of the rambling house. He might call the police.

That was it—he would call the police. But how? Go into a house near by, wake the residents, telephone headquarters that a murder had been done? Alarm the neighborhood, and identify himself with the crime? Spike was afraid, frankly and boyishly afraid—afraid of the present, and more afraid of the future.

And yet he knew that he must get in touch with the police, else the police would eventually get in touch with him. He thought then of taking the body in to headquarters; but he feared that his cab might be stopped *en route* to the city and the body discovered. They would never believe, then, that he had been bound for headquarters.

Almost before he knew that he had arrived at a decision, Spike had groped his way across the icy street and pressed the bell-button on the front door of the least unprepossessing house on the block.

For a long time there was no answer. Finally a light shone in the hall, and the skinny figure of a man, shivering violently despite the blanket-robe which enfolded him, appeared in the hallway. He flashed on the porch light from inside and peered through the glass door. Apparently reassured, he cracked the door slightly.

"Yes. What do you want?"

At sound of a human voice, Spike instantly felt easier. The fact that he could converse, that he had shed his terrible loneliness, steadied him as nothing else could have done. He was surprised at his own calmness, at the fact that there was scarcely a quaver in the voice with which he answered the man.

"I'm Spike Walters," he said with surprising quietness. "I'm a driver for the Yellow and White Taxicab Company. My cab is No. 92,381. I have a man in my cab who has been badly injured. I want to telephone to the city."

The little householder opened the door wider, and Spike entered. Cold as the house was, from the standpoint of the man within, its hold-over warmth was a godsend to Spike's thoroughly chilled body.

The little man designated a telephone on the wall, then started nervously as central answered and Spike barked a single command into the transmitter:

"Police-station, please!"

"Police?"

"Never you mind, sir," Spike told the householder. "Hello! Police!" he called to the operator.

There was a pause, then Spike went on:

"This is Spike Walters—Yellow and White Taxi Company. I'm out at No. 981 East End Avenue. There's a dead man in my cab!"

The weary voice at the other end became suddenly alive.

"A dead man!"

"Yes."

"Who is he?"

"I don't know. That's why I called you."

"When did he die? How?"

Spike controlled himself with an effort.

"Don't you understand? He has been killed—"

"The devil you say!" replied the voice at headquarters, and the little householder chimed in with a frightened squeak.

"Yes," repeated Spike painstakingly. "The man is dead—killed. It is very peculiar. I can't explain over the phone. I called up to ask you what I shall do."

"Hold connection a minute!" Spike heard a hurried whispered conversation at the other end, then the voice barked back at him: "Stay where you are—couple of officers coming, and coming fast!"

It was Dan O'Leary, night desk sergeant, who was on duty at headquarters that night, and Sergeant Dan O'Leary was a good deal of an institution on the city's force. He hopped excitedly from his desk into the office of Eric Leverage, the chief of police.

Chief Leverage, a broad-shouldered, heavy-set, bushy-eyebrowed individual, looked up from the chess-board, annoyed at this interruption of a game which had been in progress since ten o'clock that night. O'Leary grabbed a salute from thin air.

"'Scuse my botherin' ye, chief, but there's hell to pay out at East End."

O'Leary was never long at coming to the point. Leverage looked up. So, too, did the boyish, clean-shaven young man with whom he was playing chess.

"An' knowin' that Mr. Carroll was playin' chess with ye, chief—an' him naturally interested in such things—I hopped right in."

"I'll say you did," commented the chief phlegmatically. "I have you there, Carroll—dead to rights!"

O'Leary was a trifle irritated at the cold reception accorded his news.

"Ye ain't after understanding" he said slowly. "It's murder that has been done this night."

"H-m!" Carroll's slow, pleasant drawl seemed to soothe O'Leary. "Murder?"

"You said it, Mr. Carroll."

Leverage had risen. It was plain to be seen from his manner that the chess-game was forgotten. Leverage was a policeman first and a chess-player second–a very poor second. His voice, surcharged with interest, cracked out into the room.

"Spill the dope, O'Leary!"

The night desk sergeant needed no further bidding. In a few graphic words he outlined his telephone conversation with Spike Walters.

Before he finished speaking, Leverage was slipping into his enormous overcoat. He nodded to Carroll.

"How about trotting out there with me, David?"

Carroll smiled agreeably.

"Thank goodness my new coupe has a heating device, chief!"

That was all. It wasn't David Carroll's way to talk much, or to show any untoward emotion. It was Carroll's very boyishness which was his greatest asset. He had a way of stepping into a case before the principals knew he was there, and of solving it in a manner which savored not at all of flamboyance. A quiet man was Carroll, and one whose deductive powers Eric Leverage fairly worshiped.

On the slippery, skiddy journey to East End the two men–professional policeman and amateur criminologist– did not talk much. A few comments regarding the sudden advent of fiercest winter; a remark, forcedly jocular, from the chief, that murderers might be considerate enough to pick better weather for the practice of their profession– and that was all. Thus far they knew nothing about the case, and they were both too well versed in criminology to attempt a discussion of something with which they were unfamiliar.

Spike Walters saw them coming–saw their headlights splitting the frigid night. He was at the curb to meet them as they pulled up. He told his story briefly and concisely. Leverage inspected the young man closely, made note of his license number and the number of his taxi-cab. Then he turned to his companion, who had stood by, a silent and interested observer.

"S'pose you talk to him a bit, Carroll."

"I'm David Carroll," introduced the other man. "I'm connected with the police department. There's a few things you tell which are rather peculiar. Any objections to discussing them?"

In spite of himself, Spike felt a genial warming toward this boyish-faced man. He had heard of Carroll, and rather feared his prowess; but now that he was face to face with him, he found himself liking the chap. Not only that, but he was conscious of a sense of protection, as if Carroll were there for no other purpose than to take care of him, to see that he received a square deal.

"Yes, sir, Mr. Carroll, I'll be glad to tell you anything I know."

"You have said, Walters, that the passenger you picked up at the Union Station was a woman."

"Yes, sir, it was a woman."

"Are you sure?"

"Why, yes, sir. I couldn't very well be mistaken. You see–o-o-oh! You're thinking maybe it was a man in woman's clothes? Is that it, sir?"

Carroll smiled.

"What do *you* think?"

"That's impossible, sir. It was a woman–I'd swear to that."

"Pretty positive, eh?"

"Absolutely, sir. Besides, take the matter of the overcoat the–the–body has on. Even if what you think was so, sir–that it was a woman dressed up like a man–

and if he had gotten rid of the women's clothes, where would he have gotten the clothes to put on?"

"H-m! Sounds logical. How about the suit-case you said this woman had?"

"Yonder it is—right on the front beside me, where it has been all the time."

"And you tell us that between the time you left the Union Station and the time you got here a man got into the taxicab, was killed by the woman, the woman got out, and you heard nothing?"

"Yes, sir," said Spike simply. "Just that, sir."

"Rather hard to believe, isn't it?"

"Yes, sir. That's why I called the police." Chief Leverage was shivering under the impact of the winter blasts.

"S'pose we take a look at the bird, David," he suggested, nodding toward the taxi. "That might tell us something."

Carroll nodded. The men entered the taxi, and Leverage flashed a pocket-torch in the face of the dead man. Then he uttered an exclamation of surprise not unmixed with horror.

"Good Lord!"

"You know him?" questioned Carroll easily.

"Know him? I'll say I do. Why, man, that's Roland Warren!"

"Warren! Roland Warren! Not the clubman?"

"The very same one, Carroll, an' none other. Well, I'm a sonovagun! Sa-a-ay, something surely *has* been started here." He swung around on the taxi-driver. "You, Walters!"

"Yes, sir?"

"You are sure the suit-case is still in front?"

"Yes, sir."

"Well"—to Carroll—"that makes it easier. It's the woman's suit-case, and if we can't find out who she is from that, we're pretty bum, eh?"

"Looks so, Erie. You're satisfied"–this to Walters–"that that is her suit-case?"

"Absolutely. It hasn't been off the front since she handed it to me at the station."

Carroll swung the suit-case to the inside of the cab. It opened readily. Leverage kept his light trained on it as Carroll dug swiftly through the contents. Finally the eyes of the two men met. Carroll's expression was one of frank amazement; Leverage's reflected sheer unbelief.

"It can't be, Carroll!"

"Yet–it is!"

"Sufferin' wildcats!" breathed Leverage. "The suit-case ain't the woman's at all! It's Warren's!"

3
"FIND THE WOMAN"

The thing was incomprehensible, yet true. Not a single article of feminine apparel was contained in the suit-case. Not only that, but every garment therein which bore an identification mark was the property of Roland Warren, the man whose body leered at them from the floor of the taxicab.

The two detectives again inspected the suit-case. An extra suit had been neatly folded. The pockets bore the label of a leading tailor, and the name "Roland R. Warren." The tailor-made shirts and underwear bore the maker's name and Warren's initials. The handkerchiefs were Warren's. Even those articles which were without name or initials contained the same laundry-mark as those which they knew belonged to the dead man.

Carroll's face showed keen interest. This newest development had rather startled him, and made an almost irresistible appeal to his love for the bizarre in crime. The very fact that the circumstances smacked of the impossible intrigued him. He narrowed his eyes and gazed again upon the form of the dead man. Finally he nudged Leverage and designated three initials on the end of the suit-case.

"R.R.W.–Roland R. Warren!" Leverage grunted. "It's his, all right, Carroll. But just the same there ain't no such animal."

Carroll turned to the dazed Walters.

"Understand what we've just discovered, son?" he inquired mildly.

Spike's teeth were chattering with cold.

"I don't hardly understand none of it, sir. 'Cording to what I make out, that suit-case belongs to the body and not to the woman."

"Right! Now what I want to know is how that could be."

Spike shook his head dazedly.

"Lordy, Mr. Carroll, I couldn't be knowing that."

"You're sure the woman got into your cab alone?"

"Absolutely, sir. She came through the waiting-room alone, carrying that very same suit-case—"

"You're positive it was *that* suit-case?"

"Yes, sir—that is, as positive as I can be. You see I was on the lookout for a fare, but wasn't expecting one, on account of the fact that this here train was an accommodation, and folks that usually come in on it take street-cars and not a taxi. Well, the minute I seen a good-lookin', well-dressed woman comin' out the door, I sort of noticed. It surprised me first off, because I asked myself what she was doing on that train."

"You thought it was peculiar?"

"Not peculiar, exactly; but sort of—of—interesting."

"I see. Go ahead!"

"Well, she was carrying that suit-case, and she seemed in a sort of a hurry. She walked straight out of the door and toward the curb, and—"

"Did she appear to be expecting someone?"

"No, sir. I noticed that particularly. Sort of thought a fine lady like her would have someone to meet her, which is how I happened to notice that she didn't seem to expect nobody. She come right to the curb and called me. I was parked along the curb on the right side of Atlantic Avenue—headin' north, that is—and I rolled up. She handed me the suit-case and told me to drive her to No. 981 East End Avenue. I stuck the suit-case right where you got it from just now; and while I ain't sayin' nothin' about what happened back yonder in the cab, Mr. Carroll, I'll bet anything in the world that that there suit-case is the same one she carried through the waitin'-room and handed to me."

"H-m! Peculiar. You drove straight out here, Walters?"

"Straight as a bee-line, sir. Frozen stiff, I was, drivin' right into the wind eastward along East End Avenue, and I had to raise the windshield a bit because there was ice on it and I couldn't see nothin'—an' my headlights ain't any too strong."

"You didn't stop anywhere?"

"No, sir. Wait a minute—I did!"

"Where?"

"At the R.L. and T. railroad crossing, sir. I didn't see nor hear no train there, and almost run into it. It was a freight, and travelin' kinder slow. I seen the lights of the caboose and stopped the car right close to the track. I wasn't stopped more'n fifteen or twenty seconds, and just as soon as the train got by, I went on."

"But you did stand still for a few seconds?"

"Yes, sir."

"If anyone had got into or out of the cab right there, would you have heard them?"

"I don't know that I would. I was frozen stiff, like I told you, sir; and I wasn't thinking of nothin' like that. Besides, the train was makin' a noise; an' me not havin' my thoughts on nothin' but how cold I was, an' how far I had to drive, I mos' prob'ly wouldn't have noticed— although I might have."

"Looks to me," chimed in Leverage, "as if that's where the shift must have taken place; though it beats me—"

Carroll lighted a cigarette. Of the three men, he was the only one who seemed impervious to the cold. Leverage and the taxi-driver were both shivering as if with the ague. Carroll, an enormous overcoat snuggled about his neck, his hands thrust deep into his pockets, his boyish face set with interest, seemed perfectly comfortable. As a matter of fact, the unique circumstances surrounding the murder had so interested him that he had quite forgotten the weather.

"Obviously," he said to Leverage, "it's up to us to find out whether the people at this house here expected a visitor."

"You said it, David; but I haven't any doubt it was a plant, a fake address."

"I think so, too."

"Wait here." The chief started for the dark little house. "I'll ask 'em."

Three minutes later Leverage was back.

"Said nothing doing," he imparted laconically. "No one expected—no one away who would be coming back—and then wanted to know who in thunder I was. They almost dropped dead when I told 'em. No question about it, that address was a stall. This dame had something up her sleeve, and took care to see that your taxi man was given a long drive so she'd have plenty of time to croak Warren."

"Then you think she met him by arrangement, chief?"

"Looks so to me. Only thing is, where did he get in?"

"That's what is going to interest us for some time to come, I'm afraid. And now suppose we go back to town? I'll drive my car; I'll keep behind you and Walters, here. You ride together in his cab."

Walters clambered to his seat, and succeeded, after much effort, in starting his frozen motor. Leverage bulked beside him on the suit-case of the dead man. The taxi swung cityward, and immediately behind trailed Carroll in his cozy coupe.

As Carroll drove mechanically through the night, he gave himself over to a siege of intensive thought. The case seemed fraught with unusual interest. Already it had developed an overplus of extraordinary circumstances, and Carroll had a decided premonition that the road of investigation ahead promised many surprises.

There was every reason why it should. The social prominence of the dead man, the mysterious disappearance of the handsomely dressed woman—all the facts of the case pointed to an involved trail.

If it were true that the woman had entered the taxicab alone, that the man had come in later, and that the murder had been committed by the woman in the cab before reaching the railroad crossing, the thing must undoubtedly have been prearranged to the smallest fractional detail. That being the premise, it was only a logical conclusion that persons other than the woman and the dead man were involved.

Interesting—decidedly so! But there was nothing to work on. Even the suit-case clue had vanished into thin air, so far as its value to the police was concerned.

That suit-case bothered Carroll. He believed Spike's story, and was convinced that the suit-case which they had examined out on East End Avenue was the one which the woman had carried from the train to the taxicab. There again the trail of the dead man and the vanished woman crossed; else why was she carrying his suit-case?

The journey was over before he knew it. The yellow taxi turned down the alley upon which headquarters backed, and jerked to a halt before the ominous brown-stone building. Carroll parked his car at the rear, assigned someone to stand guard over the body, and the three men, Leverage carrying the suit-case, ascended the steps to the main room and thence to the chief's private office.

The warmth of the place was welcome to all of them, and in the comforting glow of a small grate fire, which nobly assisted the struggling furnace in its task of heating the spacious structure, Spike Walters seemed to lose much of the nervousness which he had exhibited since the discovery of the body. Carroll warmed his hands at the blaze, and then addressed Leverage.

"How about this case, chief?"

"How about it?"

"You want me to butt in on it?"

"*Want* you? Holy sufferin' oysters! Carroll, if you didn't work on it, I'd brain you! You're the only man in the State who could–"

"Soft-pedal the blarney," grinned Carroll. "And now–the suit-case again."

He dropped to his knees and opened the suit-case. Garment by garment he emptied it, searching for some clue, some damning bit of evidence, which might explain the woman's possession of the dead man's belongings. He found nothing. It was evident that the grip had been carefully packed for a journey of several days at least; but it was a man's suit-case, and its contents were exclusively masculine.

Carroll shrugged as he rose to his feet. He turned toward Spike Walters and laid a gentle hand on the young man's shoulder.

"Walters," he said, "I want to let you know that I believe your story all the way through. I think that Chief Leverage does, too–how about it, chief?"

"Sounds all right to me."

"But we've got to hold you for a while, my lad. It's tough, but you were the person found with the body, and we've naturally got to keep you in custody. Understand?"

"Yes, sir. It's none too pleasant, but I guess it's all right."

"We'll see that you're made comfortable, and I hope we'll be able to let you go within a day or so."

He pressed a button, and turned Walters over to one of the officers on inside duty, with instructions to see that the young taxi-driver was afforded every courtesy and comfort, and was not treated as a criminal. Spike turned at the door.

"I want to thank you–"

"That's all right, Spike!"

"You're both mighty nice fellers–especially you, Mr. Carroll. I'm for you every time!"

Carroll blushed like a schoolgirl. The door closed behind Walters, and Carroll faced Leverage.

"Next thing is the body, chief."

"Want it up here?"

"If you please."

An orderly was summoned, commands given, and within five minutes the body of the dead man was borne into the room and laid carefully on the couch. Leverage glanced inquisitively at Carroll.

"Want the coroner?"

"Surely; and you might also call in the newspapermen."

"Eh? Reporters?"

"Yes. I have a hunch, Leverage, that a great gob of sensational publicity, right now, will be of inestimable help. Meanwhile let's get busy before either the coroner or the reporters arrive."

The two detectives went over the body meticulously. Warren had been shot through the heart. Carroll bent to inspect the wound, and when he straightened his manner showed that he had become convinced of one important fact. In response to Leverage's query, he explained:

"Shot fired from mighty close," he said.

"Sure?"

"The flame from the gun has scorched his clothes. That's proof enough."

"In the taxi, eh?"

"Possibly."

"But the driver would have heard."

"He probably would; but he didn't."

"Ye-e-es."

Carroll resumed his inspection of the body, examining every detail of figure and raiment; and while he worked he talked.

"You know something about this chap?"

"More or less. He's prominent socially; belongs to clubs, and all that sort of thing. Has money—real money. Bachelor—lives alone. Has a valet, and all that kind of rot. Owns his car. Golfer—tennis-player—huntsman. Popular with women—and men, too, I believe. About thirty-three years old."

"Business?"

"None. He's one of the few men in town who don't work at something. That's how I happen to know so much about him. A chap who's different from other fellows is usually worth knowing something about."

"Right you are! But that sort of a man—you'd hardly think he'd be the victim of—hello, what's this?"

Carroll had been going through the dead man's wallet. He rose to his feet, and as he did so Leverage saw that the purse was stuffed with bills of large denomination—a very considerable sum of money. But apparently Carroll was not interested in the money; in his hand he held a railroad-ticket and a small purple Pullman check.

"What's the idea?" questioned Leverage.

"Brings us back to the woman again," replied Carroll, with peculiar intensity.

"How so?"

"He was planning to take a trip with her."

Leverage glanced at the other man with an admixture of skepticism and wonder.

"How did you guess that?"

"I didn't guess it. It's almost a sure thing. At least, it is pretty positive that he was not planning to go alone."

"Yes? Tell me how you know."

Carroll extended his hand.

"See here—a ticket for a drawing-room to New York, and *one* railroad-ticket!"

"Yes, but—"

"Two railroad-tickets are required for possession of the drawing-room," he said quietly. "Warren had only one. It is clear, then, that the holder of the missing ticket was going to accompany him; so what we have to do now—"

"Is to find the other railroad-ticket," finished Leverage dryly. "Which isn't any lead-pipe cinch, I'd say!"

4
CARROLL HAS A VISITOR

Carroll gazed intently upon the face of the dead man. There was a half quizzical light in the detective's eyes as he spoke, apparently to no one.

"I've often thought," he said, "in a case like this, how much simpler things would be if the murdered man could talk."

"H-m!" rejoined the practical Leverage. "If he could, he wouldn't be dead."

"Perhaps you're right. And following that to a logical conclusion, if he were not dead *we* wouldn't be particularly interested in what he had to say."

"All of which ain't got a heap to do with the fact that your work is cut out for you, Carroll. You're dead sure about that ticket dope, ain't you? I ain't used to traveling in drawing-rooms myself."

"It's straight enough, Leverage. The railroad company won't allow a single passenger to occupy a drawing-room— that is, they demand two tickets. If you, for instance, were traveling alone, and desired a drawing-room, you'd be compelled to have two tickets for yourself. That being so, it is plain that Warren there didn't intend making this trip to New York alone. If he had, he would have had the two tickets along with the drawing-room check. I am certain that two tickets were bought, because the railroad men won't sell a drawing-room with a single ticket. It is obvious, then, that he bought two tickets and gave the other one to the person who was to make the trip with him."

"The woman, of course!"

"What woman?"

"The woman in the fur coat—the one who got into the taxicab."

"Perhaps; but she came in on the accommodation train after the New York train was due to leave. The fast train was late."

"So was the accommodation. They are due to make connection."

"That's true. If we can find that ticket—"

"We'll have found the woman, and when we find her the case will end."

"Probably—"

The door opened, and Sergeant O'Leary entered.

"The coroner, sorr—him an' a reporter from each av the mornin' papers."

"Show the coroner in first," ordered Carroll. "Let the newspapermen wait."

"Yis, sorr. They seem a bit impatient, sorr. They say they're holdin' up the city edition for the news, sorr."

"Very good. Tell them Chief Leverage says the story is worth waiting for."

The coroner—a short, thick-set man—entered and heard the story from Leverage's lips. He made a cursory examination and nodded to Carroll.

"Inquest in the morning, Mr. Carroll. Meanwhile, I reckon you want to let them newspapermen in."

The two reporters entered and listened popeyed to the story. They telephoned a bulletin to their offices, and were assured of an hour's leeway in phoning in the balance of the story. They were quivering with excitement over what promised to be, from a newspaper standpoint, the juiciest morsel of sensational copy with which the city had been blessed for some time.

To them Carroll recounted the story as he knew it, concealing nothing.

"This is a great space-eating story," he told them in their own language—the jargon of the fourth estate—"and the more it eats the better it'll be for me. We want publicity on this case—all you can hand out big chunks of it. We want to know who that woman was. The way I figure it, this city is going to get a jolt at breakfast. Everyone is going to be comparing notes. Out of that mass of gossip we may get some valuable information. Get that?"

"We do. Space in the morning edition will be limited, but by evening, and the next morning—oh, baby!"

They took voluminous notes and telephoned in enough additional information to keep the city rooms busy. When they would have gone, Carroll stopped them.

"Either of you chaps know anything of Warren's personal history?"

The elder of the two nodded.

"I do. Know him personally, in fact. I've played golf with him. Pretty nice sort."

"Rich, isn't he?"

"Reputed to be. Never works; spends freely—not ostentatiously, but liberally. Pretty fine sort of a chap. It's a damned shame!"

"How about his relations with women?"

The reporter hesitated and glanced guiltily at the dead body.

"That's rather strong—"

"It's not going beyond here, unless I find it necessary. I've played clean with you boys. Suppose you do the same with me."

"We-e-ell"—reluctantly—"he was rather much of a rounder. Nothing coarse about him, but he never was one to resist a woman. Rather the reverse, in fact."

"Ever been mixed up in a scandal?"

"Not publicly. He's friendly with a good many men— and with their wives. A dozen, I guess; but the husbands invite him to their homes, so I don't suppose there could be anything in the gossip. You see, folks are always too eager to talk about a man in his position and whatever woman he happens to be friendly with. And anyway, there hasn't been nearly so much talk about him since his engagement was announced."

"He is engaged?"

"Why, yes."

"To a girl in this city!"

"Sure! I thought you knew that. Dandy girl–Hazel Gresham. You've heard of Garry Gresham? It's his kid sister."

"So-o! How long has this engagement been known?"

"Couple of months. Pretty soft on both sides; he's got money and so has she. She's a good scout, too, even if she is a kid."

"How old?"

"Hardly more than twenty; but her family seemed to welcome the match. Warren and Garry Gresham were pretty good friends. Warren was about thirty-three or thirty-four, you know. Gossip had it that the family was going to object because of the difference in ages, but they didn't."

Carroll was silent for a moment.

"Nothing else about him you think might prove interesting?"

"No-o."

"And your idea of the murderer, after what you've heard?"

"The woman in the taxicab killed him."

"When did he get in?"

The reporter threw back his head and laughed.

"What is this–a game? If I knew that I'd have your job, Mr. Carroll. The dame killed him, all right; and when we find out how she did it, and when, and how he got in and she got out, we'll have a whale of a story!"

"No theories as to the identity of this woman, have you?"

"Nary one. A chap like Warren–bachelor, unencumbered–is liable to know a heap of 'em. From what you tell me of the tickets–from the fact that she was going away with him, I sort of figure you might do a little social investigating and discover what woman might have been going off with him."

Eric Leverage had been listening intently. His mind, never swift to work, yet worked surely. His big voice boomed into the conversation:

"Carroll?"

"Yes?"

"This young fellow says Miss Gresham's family didn't have no objections to the marriage. It just occurred to me to ask him is he *sure*?"

The reporter flushed.

"Why, no, chief; not sure. You never can be sure about things like that; but so far as the public knew—"

"That's it, exactly. How do we know, though, but what they were sore as a pup over it, and just kept their traps closed because they didn't want any gossip? S'posin' they were trying to break things off, an' makin' it pretty uncomfortable for the girl? S'pose that, eh?"

"Yes," argued the reporter. "Suppose all of that. Where does it get you?"

"It gets you just here"—Leverage talked slowly, heavily, tapping his spatulate fingers on the table to emphasize his points—"we know this bird was going to elope with some skirt. All right! Now I ask this—why go all around the block, looking for someone he might have been mixed up with, when the woman a man is most likely to elope with is the girl he's engaged to marry?"

Silence—several seconds of it. Carroll spoke:

"Miss Gresham, you mean?"

"Sure, David—sure! I'm not sayin' she was the woman, mind you. I'm not sayin' anything except that if I'm right in thinkin' that maybe her folks weren't as crazy about this guy Warren as they seemed—if I'm right in that, maybe they was plannin' to take matters in their own hands and elope."

"It's possible."

"Sure, it's possible, and—"

"But, chief," interrupted the reporter who had done most of the talking, "why should Miss Gresham kill Warren?"

"I didn't say she did, did I?"

"If she was the woman in the taxi—"

"If! Sure—*if!* All I mentioned that for was to show you we might as well start thinking close to home before we go to beatin' through the bushes to follow a cold trail."

The reporters left, and Carroll smiled at Leverage.

"Good idea, Eric—about Miss Gresham."

"'Tain't a hunch," said Leverage. "It just made good talkin'."

"I'm glad you did it, anyway."

"What is thare about it that you like?"

"Those newspaper chaps will play it up. Maybe they won't intend to, but they'll play it up, just the same; and it won't take us long either to connect Miss Gresham with the crime or to link up an iron-clad alibi for her."

"H-m! Not bad! You know, Carroll"—and Leverage smiled frankly—"I'm always makin' these fine suggestions an' pullin' good stunts, an' never knowin' whether they're good or not until somebody tells me."

"A good many folks are like that, Eric, but they don't admit it afterward."

"Neither do I—publicly."

Leverage rose and yawned.

"It's me for the hay, Carroll. I'm played out; and I have a hunch that to-morrow I'm going to be busy as seven little queen bees—and you, too."

Carroll reached for his overcoat.

"A little bit of thinking things over isn't going to hurt me, either. Good night!"

Thirty minutes later Carroll reached his apartment, and a half-hour after that he was sleeping soundly. The following morning he waked "all over," as was his habit, and turned his eyes to gaze through the window. During the night the sleety drizzle had ceased, and the sun streamed with brilliant coldness upon a city which shone in a glare of ice. Leafless trees stretched their ice-covered tentacles into the cold, penetrating air; pedestrians and horses slipped on the glassy pavements; automobiles either skidded dangerously or set up an incessant rattle with their chains.

Carroll glanced at his watch. It showed nine o'clock. He started with surprise. Then he reached for the newspapers on the table at the side of his bed, and spread open the front pages.

They had evidently been made up anew with the breaking of the Warren murder story. Eight-column streamers shrieked at him from both front pages. He read the stories through, and smiled with satisfaction. Just as he had anticipated, both reporters, hungry for some definite clue upon which to work, had seized upon the possibility of Hazel Gresham being the mysterious woman in the taxicab. Not that they said so openly, but they said enough to make the public know that the detectives in charge of the case were likely to investigate her movements on the previous night.

Carroll stepped into a shower, then dressed quickly and ate a light breakfast served him by his maid, Freda. Before he finished, the doorbell rang, and Freda announced that there was a lady to see him.

"A lady?"

Freda shrugged.

"She ain't bane nothin' but a girl, sir, Mr. Carroll—just a little girl."

"Show her in."

In two minutes Freda returned, and behind her came the visitor. Carroll concealed a smile at sight of her. She was a little thing—sixteen or seventeen years old, he judged—a fluffy, blond girl quivering with vivacity; the type of girl who is desperately reaching for maturity, entirely forgetful of the charms of her adolescence. He rose and bowed in a serious, courtly manner.

"You wish to see me?"

"Yes, sir, I *do*. Is *this* Mr. Carroll–the famous detective?"

"I am David Carroll–yes."

She inspected him with frank approval.

"Why, you don't look any more than a boy! I thought you were old and had whiskers–and–and–everything horrid."

"I'm glad you're pleasantly surprised. What can I do for you?"

"Oh, it isn't what you can do for me–it's what I can do for you!"

"And that is?"

"I came to tell you all about this terrible Warren murder case."

"*You* came to tell *me* about it?"

"Why, yes," she retorted smilingly. "You see, I know just *heaps* about the whole thing!"

5
MISS EVELYN ROGERS

Carroll was more than amused; he was keenly interested. He motioned his visitor to a chair and seated himself opposite, regarding her quizzically.

She was not exactly the type of person he had anticipated encountering in a murder investigation. From the tip of her pert little hat to the toes of her ultra-fashionable shoes she was expressive of the independent rising generation—a generation wiser in the ways of the world than that from which it was sprung—a generation strangely bereft of genuine youth, yet charming in an entirely modern and unique manner.

She was obviously a young person of italics, a human exclamation-point, enthusiastic, irrepressible. She sat fidgeting in her chair, trying her best to convince the detective that she was a woman grown.

"I'm Evelyn Rogers," she gushed. "I'm the sister of Naomi Lawrence—you know her, of *course*. She's one of the city's social leaders. Of course, she's kind of frumpy and terribly old. She must be—why, I suppose she's every bit of thirty! And that's simply *awful!*"

"I'm thirty-eight," smiled Carroll.

"No?"

"Yes, indeed."

"Well, you don't look it. You don't look a day over twenty-two, and I think men who are really grown up and yet look like boys are simply *adorable!* I do, really. And I simply *despise* boys of twenty-two who try to look like thirty-eight. Don't you?"

"M-m! Not always."

"Well, *I* do! They're always putting on airs and trying to make us girls think they're full-grown. I just simply haven't time to waste with them. I feel so *old!*"

"I haven't a doubt of it, Miss Rogers. And now–I believe you came to tell me something about the Warren case?"

"Oh, yes, indeed–just *lots!* But do you know"–she stared at him with frank approval–"I'm terribly tickled with the way you look. You may not believe it, but I've always been *atrociously* in love with you."

"No?"

"Yes, indeed! You're such a *wonderful* man–having your name in the papers all the time. Oh, I've read about everything you've done! That's how I learned so much about detectiving–or isn't that what you call it?"

"Detecting?"

"That's it. You know I always was simply *incorrigible* in making up words when I couldn't think of the right one. Don't you think it's a lot of trouble sometimes– thinking of just the right word in the right place?"

"Sometimes. But about the Warren case?"

"Oh, yes, certainly! I'm always getting off my subject, ain't I? I mean–am I not? Bother grammar, anyway. It's a terrible bore, don't you think?"

"Yes, Miss Rogers. And now–"

"Back to that awful crime again, aren't you? It's simply sugary the way you great detectives stick to one subject. I can do it, too, when I have to. I took some lessons once in power of will–concentration and all that sort of thing. It made me feel wickedly old; but I learned a great deal about keeping my mind on one subject all the time. You know, it doesn't matter what you concentrate on–even if it's only making biscuits, or something messy and domestic like that–it does you good. It trains you not to waste words, and to store up your mental energy, and all that sort of thing. And all the time I was studying that course, I was thinking how perfectly glorious modern science is. Just suppose Shakespeare had been able to concentrate like us moderns can! His plays would have been utterly *marvelous*, wouldn't they?"

"I suppose they would. And now let's try concentrating on the Warren case."

"That's what I've been leading up to. You see, I knew Mr. Warren very well. In fact, he was awfully friendly with me. To tell you the strict truth, and absolutely in confidence, I really believe he was in love with me!"

"No?"

"Yes, truly! We women have a way of knowing when a man is in love with us. He used to be around at the house all the time. Of course, he pretended that he came around because he liked Sis and Gerald—"

"Gerald?"

"That's Mr. Lawrence. He's my brother-in-law—Sis's husband. Insufferably old-timy. Don't think of anything but business. Used to look at me through his horn-rimmed glasses and say I was entirely too young to be receiving attentions from a man as old as Mr. Warren; but he didn't know. I'm not young, really, you know. Of course, I'm not twenty yet, but a girl can be under twenty and yet be a woman, can't she?"

"Yes"—dryly—"especially after she learns to concentrate."

"And as intimately as I knew Roland—that's Mr. Warren, you know—of course I didn't call him Roland to his face. Not that he didn't want me to, but then Sis and Gerald would have disapproved—old frumps! Knowing him so intimately, and really believing that he was in love with me—although, of course, the minute he became engaged to Hazel Gresham I didn't even flirt with him any more—not the least little tiny harmless bit well, I find it excruciatingly hard to believe that he is dead!"

"He is—quite. We're trying to discover who killed him."

"I know it. That's what I came to see you about."

"So you did. I'd quite forgotten—"

"You ought to learn to concentrate, Mr. Carroll. It's really ridiculously easy after you've studied it a little bit. Now if I had been you, and you had been I–me–I never would have forgotten what you came to see me about. Of course, I know you didn't forget, really; but the chances are that you were interested talking, and absolutely failed to remember that poor boy."

"What poor boy?"

"Roland Warren."

Carroll with difficulty concealed a smile.

"I see! And now that I've remembered him again, suppose you tell me what you know about him and the case?"

"It's principally about what I read in the papers this morning. Really, Mr. Carroll, there ought to be a law against newspapers printing such ridiculous things!"

"As what, for instance?"

"That thing they had in there this morning. Why, the way they mentioned Hazel Gresham, you'd have thought that they thought *she* was the woman who killed Roland– the woman in the taxicab."

Carroll's eyes narrowed slightly. The faint smile still played about his lips.

"You don't think she was?"

"Oh, Mr. Carroll! Please, *please*, don't be so irresistibly *absurd*! Why in the world should Hazel kill the man she was engaged to?"

"I don't know."

"And besides, what does *she* know about killing someone? That is the most bizarre idea I have ever heard in all my life. Besides, she couldn't have killed him, anyway."

"Why not?"

"Even if she'd wanted to, she couldn't; and I'm sure she didn't want to. Not that I think Roland Warren was the finest man in the world, or anything like that. Of course, I do believe he was interested in me, and that made me know him pretty well; but still he was an awfully nice boy, and I'm sure Hazel was very much in love with him. So even if she could have killed him, she wouldn't, would she?"

"I hope not; but you said she *couldn't*. What did you mean by that?"

"I mean that nobody can be in two places at one time. Although I did read a funny article in the Sunday magazine section of one of the big newspapers, last year, which said that—"

"If Miss Gresham had been with Mr. Warren last night at midnight—she would have been in two places at one time!"

"Why, yes—and that's not possible; so, of course, she—"

"What makes you think that, Miss Rogers!"

"Think what?"

"That Miss Gresham was not with Mr. Warren at midnight last night?"

"Why," answered Evelyn Rogers simply, "I *know* she wasn't—that's all."

"You *know*?"

"Yes, indeed—beyond the what-you-call-'em of a doubt."

"How do you know that?"

"It's very simple," she explained casually. "She was with me all night."

Carroll gazed at the girl before him with new interest. Out of her chatter he had at last garnered one important fact. His mind, trained to seize upon the vital and instantly discard the inconsequential, clutched the bit of information, and turned it over. From the first Carroll had scouted the idea that the dead man's fiancée might have been responsible for his death; but still it was a line of investigation which demanded examination, and his pretty young visitor was making that road exceedingly simple. He injected all the warmth of his friendly, sunny nature in the smile which he bestowed upon her.

"You have helped me tremendously with that piece of information, Miss Rogers."

"I don't see how, particularly. No one with any sense—provided they knew Hazel, of course—could even imagine her killing anyone, and least of all an adorable boy like Roland. She was so much in love with him!"

"Of course, I haven't the pleasure of Miss Gresham's acquaintance."

"Of course not. You'll have to meet her, though. She's a darling! Naturally, she's all broken up this morning because her wedding date was all set. Now all her plans have gone smash, and she really was *terribly* fond—"

"You say you spent the night with Miss Gresham?"

"Certainly, and—"

"Where?"

"At her house."

"And you are sure she was there all night?"

"Of course! We slept in the same bed—and that's certainly proof enough, isn't it?"

"I suppose so."

"You *suppose*? My goodness gracious! Don't you know?"

"Well—yes. If you're sure—"

"Why, my dear Mr. Carroll, we didn't even actually go to bed until a quarter before twelve. At ten o'clock we made some waffles downstairs—Hazel has just bought a perfectly *darling* aluminum electric waffle-iron. It makes the most toothsome waffles—all crisp and everything. And you know when you use aluminum you don't need any grease, so that makes the waffles much nicer. I'm getting horribly domestic since Hazel became engaged, because she is learning—"

"And after you made the waffles?"

"Oh! After that we went up-stairs to her room, and put on our kimonos, and had a heart-to-heart talk. I can't tell you what we talked about, because sometimes—well, it was atrociously risqué—as women will, you know, and—"

"At a quarter before twelve you were still sitting up talking, and you had your kimonos on?"

"Yes, and–oh, you just ought to see Hazel's new kimono–pink *crepe de chine*, trimmed with satin. She looks simply ravishing in it. I told Sis I wanted one like it, but–"

"And then you went to bed?"

"Yes, just about then."

"You are sure Miss Gresham didn't get up!"

"Oh, I'm positive she didn't! I didn't get to sleep until after one o'clock, anyway, and I would have known."

"You've given me some valuable information, Miss Rogers; and I'll see to it that the newspapers correct any impression they may have left that Miss Gresham might have been connected with the crime. Meanwhile"–he rose–"I'm a bit overdue down at headquarters; so if you'll excuse me–"

Evelyn Rogers rose and stood before him. Her pretty little face was eager.

"I've really helped you, Mr. Carroll?"

"Enormously."

"Well, I wonder–you know I'm just fiendishly anxious to be helpful in the world–I wonder if you'd let me help you some more?"

"I'd be delighted."

"Would you *really*?"

"Really!"

"And I can come to you any time to talk things over?"

"Whenever you get ready."

She clapped her hands.

"That's simply *exquisite*! You know, Mr. Carroll, I'm just simply crazy about you! I always have been, but I'm more so now than ever–just *hopelessly*!"

"Thank you."

She made her way to the door. There she turned, and there was a peculiar light in her eyes.

"Mr. Carroll!"

"Yes?"

"I wish you had been nineteen years old just now."

"Why?"

"Because," she flashed, "if you had been nineteen years old when I told you what I did, you would have kissed me!"

6
REGARDING ROLAND WARREN

For a long time after Evelyn departed, Carroll remained seated, puffing amusedly on the cigar which followed his matutinal cigarette. Time had been long since the detective had come in contact with so much youthful spontaneity, and he found the experience refreshing. Then he rose and would have left the apartment for headquarters, but again Freda announced a caller.

"Another young lady?" questioned Carroll.

"No, sir. It bane young feller."

"Show him in."

The visitor entered, and Carroll found himself gazing into the level eyes of a slightly disheveled and obviously excited young man of about twenty-eight years of age. The man was slight of stature, but every nervous gesture bespoke wiriness.

"Are you Mr. Carroll?"

"Yes."

"I'm Gresham—Garrison Gresham."

"A-a-ah! Won't you be seated!"

"Yes. I came to have a talk with you."

Carroll seated himself opposite his caller. Then he nodded.

"You came to see me?"

"About the Warren case."

"You know something about it?"

"Yes!" The young man seemed to bite the word. "I do."

"What?"

"You're in charge of the case, aren't you?"

"Yes."

"You've seen this morning's papers?"

"I have."

"Well, they're rotten—absolutely rotten. They don't say it in so many words, but the impression they create is that my sister, Hazel, was the woman in the taxi who killed Roland Warren. It's a damned lie!"

The young man was growing more excited. Carroll put out a restraining hand.

"I quite agree with you, my friend—it *was* a pretty rotten impression to create; but I shall see that all doubt is removed from the mind of the public when this afternoon's papers appear. I have just learned that your sister has an ironclad alibi."

"You have already learned that?"

"Yes."

Gresham leaned forward eagerly.

"What makes you sure—that she did not—was not—"

"Suppose I question you—if you have no objections."

"Fire away."

"Where was your sister at midnight last night?"

"At home."

"Alone? I mean was anyone besides your family there?"

"Yes," replied Gresham, showing surprise at Carroll's evident knowledge of facts.

"Who?"

"Evelyn Rogers spent the night with her. Evelyn's a seventeen-year-old kid who has had what I believe you call a crush on my sister. They were together in that house from ten o'clock last night, or earlier, until this morning. And if you don't believe that—"

"But I do. I have just had a visit from Miss Rogers, and she told me exactly what you have just repeated; so I'm pretty well satisfied that your sister had nothing whatever to do with the affair. I will take pains to see that this evening's papers make that quite clear."

Gresham rose. A load seemed to have dropped from his shoulders.

"That's white of you, Carroll! I appreciate it."

"Not at all. I have no desire to cause annoyance or inconvenience where it is unnecessary. And Miss Rogers told me, with great attention to detail, just why and how it was impossible for your sister to have been anywhere except at home last night."

"Evelyn's considerable of a brick, in spite of the fact that she's more or less minus in the upper story. And now, if you're really satisfied, I'll be going."

The two men walked to the door together. They were about of a height; Carroll slightly the heavier of the two.

"You've no idea as to the identity of the woman in the taxicab, have you, Gresham?"

"No. Have you?"

"None whatever; though I fancy something ought to develop in the near future. The city is discussing it pretty freely?"

"The town's wild about it. They don't understand anything. It's tough on my sister. Hazel is only a kid, and I think she was in love with Warren. Well, good day, Carroll." He extended a firm hand. "Any time I can be of any help–"

"Thanks, Gresham."

Five minutes after Gresham's departure, Carroll was in his car, headed for the police-station. He turned the case over and over in a keen, analytic mind which had been refreshed by a night of untroubled sleep.

There were a good many features about it which puzzled him considerably. While he had not expected that the trail of the mysterious midnight woman would lead to the fiancée of the dead man, the sudden dissipation of that as a clue rather threw him off his balance. He had reached the end of a trail almost before setting foot upon it.

Thus far he had refused to allow himself to be worried by the strangest feature of the case–the appearance of the dead body in a taxicab which, according to its driver's story, could not have been other than empty. It was always easy to explain the disappearance of a person from an automobile; but, he figured, it was patently impossible to enter one without the driver's knowledge.

He reached headquarters and closeted himself with Leverage. They plunged at once into a discussion of that phase of the case.

"There are only two things which could have happened," said the chief of police slowly. "One is that someone croaked that bird Warren and shoved him into the cab while the woman was ridin' in it. The other is that he slipped into the cab and she killed him. While I ain't jumpin' on no set ideas, I have a hunch that the last one is right."

"Why?"

"Because the other–that idea of puttin' a dead body into a cab without the driver knowing it–it just naturally ain't possible."

"Then you are quite convinced, Leverage, that Walters did *not* know anything about it?"

"Now, say, Carroll, that's putting it up to me rather strong; but since you're asking, I'm here to say that I believe the kid. Of course it's possible that he was in on the deal–but I'm betting Liberty bonds against Russian rubles that he'd have slipped somewhere if that had been the case. Nobody that's in on a murder deal is going to frame a lie that sticks his bean as close to a noose as Walter's would be if he's not tellin' the truth!"

"Sounds reasonable; and yet–"

"I'm surprised at you suspectin' the kid."

"I don't suspect him."

"But you said–"

"We can't overlook anything–that's what I said. It's what I was driving at, anyway. So far, Walters is the only tangible clue we've had to work with. As I told you, the Hazel Gresham trail died a-borning. The kid who came to see me this morning cleared her; and then her brother came along right afterward, red-hot over the insinuations against his sister in the papers. As matters stand now, there's nothing to tie to but Spike Walters."

"I'm glad you're handling it," said Leverage fervently. "And as you are, I'm making so bold as to ask what you're going to do next?"

"A little general inquiring. You can help me on that. For one thing, I want to get hold of every bit of dope I can regarding Warren—who he was, where he came from, what he did, the size of his bank deposits, his business connections, his social life, and especially every morsel of gossip that's ever been circulated about him in connection with women."

"H-m! You think this dame was a society sort?"

"Probably. He was undoubtedly going away with her; and a man of his stamp doesn't often elope with a woman of the other type."

"True enough! Well, I'll get you what dope I can."

"I want it all. I'm afraid this is going to resolve itself into a contest of elimination. The city is buzzing about the case to-day, and it ought to be pretty easy to get hold of a world of gossip concerning Warren's love-affairs—provided he had any. Everybody's concerned over the identity of that woman, and every woman Warren has ever been mixed up with, even in the most innocuous way, is going to be dragged into the case."

Carroll made his way from headquarters direct to the consolidated railroad ticket office. He introduced himself to the chief clerk and stated his business. The other showed keen interest.

"The tickets were sold to him in this office, Mr. Carroll. This young man here sold them."

Carroll smiled genially at the skinny young chap who bustled forward importantly, proud of his temporary spotlight position.

"You sold some tickets to Roland Warren?"

"Yes, sir."

"When?"

"Day before yesterday."

"You are sure it was Mr. Warren?"

"Yes, sir. I have known him by sight for a longtime."

"About the tickets–what did he buy?"

"Two tickets and a drawing-room on No. 29 for New York–due to leave at 11.55 last night."

"You're sure he bought *two* tickets and a drawing-room? Or was it one ticket?"

"It had to be two. We can't sell a drawing-room unless the purchaser has double transportation."

"You delivered both tickets to him personally?"

"Yes, sir–gave them both to him."

From the ticket office Carroll went back to headquarters, and from there to the coroner's office, and, accompanied by that dignitary, to the undertaking establishment where the body was being kept under police guard. Nothing had yet been touched. The inquest had resulted in a verdict of "death by violence, inflicted by a revolver in the hands of a person unknown."

Carroll again ran through the man's pockets. In a vest pocket he discovered what he sought. He took the trunk check to the Union Station, and through his police badge secured access to the baggage-room. The trunk was not there. He compared checks with the baggage-master, and learned that the trunk had duly gone to New York. He left orders for it to be returned to the city.

From there he went to the office of the division superintendent, and left a half-hour later, after an exchange of telegrams between the superintendent and the conductor of the train for New York, which informed him that the drawing-room engaged by Warren had been unoccupied, nor had there been an attempt on the part of anyone to secure possession of it. Also that the only berth purchased on the train had been at a small-town stop about four o'clock in the morning.

Obviously, then, the person who was to share the drawing-room with Warren, and for whom the second ticket had been bought, had never boarded the train. The trail had doubled back again to the woman in the taxicab.

It was not until two o'clock in the afternoon that Carroll returned to headquarters. He found Leverage ready with his report.

"For one thing," said the chief, "there isn't a doubt that Warren was getting ready to leave town–and for good."

"How so?"

Leverage checked over his list.

"First, he had sublet his apartment. Second, he had with him eleven hundred dollars in cash. Third, he left his automobile with a dealer here to be sold, and did not place an order for any other car. And fourth–" Leverage paused impressively.

"Yes–and fourth?"

"He fired his valet yesterday!"

7
THE VALET TALKS

There was a triumphant ring to Leverage's statement that the dead man's valet had been discharged at some time during the twenty-four hours which immediately preceded the killing. It was as if his instinct recognized a combination of circumstances which could not be ignored. Carroll looked up interestedly.

"Have you talked to this fellow?"

"No. I figured I'd better leave that phase of it to you; but I'm having him watched. Cartwright is on the job. Right now the man is at his boarding-place on Larson Street."

Carroll started for the door.

"Let's go," he suggested laconically.

It was but a few minutes' drive from headquarters to the boarding-house of Roland Warren's former valet. Carroll parked his car at the curb and inspected the place closely from the outside.

There was little architectural beauty to recommend the house. It was a rambling, dilapidated, two-story structure, sadly in need of paint and repairs, and bespeaking occupancy by a family none too well blessed with the better things of existence. They proceeded to the door and rang the bell. A slatternly woman answered their summons, and Leverage addressed her:

"We wish to see William Barker, please."

"William Barker?"

"Yes. I believe he moved here yesterday."

"Oh, that feller!" The woman started inside. "Wait a minute," she said crossly, and shut the door in their faces.

While they stood waiting, Leverage glanced keenly up and down the street, and his eye lighted on the muscular figure of Cartwright, the plainclothes man, shivering in the partial shelter of an alley across the way. The policeman signaled them that all was well, and resumed his vigil. At that minute the door opened and the woman reappeared.

"He ain't home!" she said, and promptly closed the door again.

Carroll looked at Leverage and Leverage looked at Carroll. Leverage crossed the street and interrogated Cartwright.

"The landlady says he's out, Cartwright. How about it?"

"Bum steer, chief! The bird's there—I'll bet my silk shirt on it!"

Leverage recrossed the street and reported to Carroll.

"You're pretty sure Cartwright has the straight dope!"

"Sure thing," said the chief. "He's one of the most reliable men on the force, and when he says a thing, he knows it."

Carroll stroked his beardless chin. There was a hard, calculating light in his eyes—eyes which alternated between a soft, friendly blue and a steely gray. Finally he looked up at Leverage.

"What's your idea, Eric?"

"About him sendin' word he was out when we know he ain't?"

"Exactly."

"It looks darn funny to me, Carroll! 'Pears like he didn't want to discuss the affair with us."

"He don't know who we are."

"He can guess pretty well. Any guy with a head on his shoulders knows the valet of a murdered man is going to be quizzed by the police."

"Good! Come on."

Carroll put a firm hand on the knob and turned it. Then he stepped into the dingy reception hall, followed by the city's chief of police.

At the sound of visitors, the angular frame of the boarding-house-keeper appeared in the doorway, her eyes flashing antagonistically. Leverage turned back the lapel of his coat and disclosed the police badge.

"Listen here, lady," he said in a voice whose very softness brooked no opposition; "that bird Barker is here, and we're going to see him. Police business! Where's his room?"

The woman's face grew ashen.

"What's he been doin'?" she quavered. "What's he been up to now?"

"What's he been up to before this?" countered Leverage.

"I don't know anything about him. Swear to Gawd I don't! He just come here yesterday an' took a room. Paid cash in advance."

"He's in his room, ain't he?"

"What if he is? He told me to tell anybody who come along that he was out. I didn't know you was cops. Oh, I hope there ain't nothin' goin' to ruin the reputation of this place! There ain't a woman in town who runs a decenter place than this."

"Nobody's going to know anything," reassured Carroll, "provided you keep your own tongue between your teeth. Now take us to Barker's room."

The boarding-house-keeper led the way up a flight of dark and twisting stairs, along a musty hall. She paused before a door at the far end.

"There it is, sirs—and—"

"You go downstairs," whispered Carroll. "If we should find you trying to listen at the keyhole—"

His manner made it unnecessary to finish the threat. The woman departed, fluttering with excitement. Leverage's hand found the knob, and Carroll nodded briefly. The door was flung open, and the two men entered.

"What the—"

The occupant of the room leaped to his feet and stood staring, his face gone pasty white, his demeanor one of terror, which Carroll could see he was fighting to control. Leverage closed the door gently and gazed at the man upon whom they had called.

William Barker was not a large man; neither was he small. He was one of those men of medium height, whose physique deceives everyone save the anatomical expert. To the casual observer his weight would have been catalogued at about a hundred and forty. At a glance Carroll knew that it was nearer a hundred and eighty. Normal breadth of shoulder was more than made up for by unusual depth of chest. Ready-made trousers bulged with the enormous muscular development of calf and thigh. The face, clean-shaven, was sullen with the fear inspired by the sudden entrance of Carroll and Leverage; and there was more than a hint of evil in it. As they watched, the sullenness of expression was supplanted by a leer, and then by a mask of professional placidity–the bovine expression which one expects to find in the average specimen of masculine hired help.

The man's demeanor was a combination of abjectness and hostility. He was plainly frightened, yet striving to appear at ease.

Carroll and Leverage maintained silence. Barker fidgeted nervously, and finally, when the strain became too great, burst out with:

"Who are you fellers? Whatcha want?"

Carroll spoke softly.

"William Barker?"

"What if that is my name?"

Carroll's hands spread wide.

"Just wanted to be sure, that's all. You *are* William Barker?"

"An' what if I am? What you got to do with that?"

Carroll showed his badge.

"And this gentleman," he finished, designating Leverage, "is chief of police."

Barker's voice came back to him in a half whine, half snarl.

"I ain't done nothin'—"

"Nobody has accused you yet."

"Well, when you bust in on a feller like this—"

Carroll seated himself, and Leverage followed suit. He motioned Barker to a chair.

"Let's talk things over," he suggested mildly.

"Ain't nothin' to talk over."

"You're William Barker, aren't you?"

"I ain't said I ain't, have I?"

Carroll's eyes grew a bit harder. His voice cracked out: "What's your name?"

Barker met his gaze; then the eyes of the ex-valet shifted.

"William Barker," he answered almost unintelligibly.

"Very good! Now, sit down, William."

William seated himself with ill grace. Carroll spoke again, but this time the softness had returned to his tones. His manner approached downright friendliness.

"We came here to talk with you, Barker," he said frankly. "We don't know a thing about your connection with this case; but we do know that you were valet to Roland Warren, and therefore must possess a great deal of information about him which no one else could possibly have. All we want is to learn what you know about this tragedy—what you know and what you think."

Barker raised his head. For a long time he stared silently at Carroll.

"I don't know who you are," he remarked at length; "but you seem to be on the level."

"I am on the level," returned Carroll quietly. "My name is David Carroll—"

"O-o-oh! So *you're* David Carroll?" The query was a sincere tribute.

"Yes, I'm Carroll, and I'm working on the Warren case. I don't want to cause trouble for anyone, but there are certain facts which I must learn. You can tell me some of them. No person who is innocent has the slightest thing to fear from me. And so–Barker–if you have nothing to conceal, I'd advise that you talk frankly."

"I ain't got nothin' to conceal. What made you think I had?"

"I don't think so. I don't think anything definite at this stage of the game. I want to find out what you know."

"I don't know nothin', either."

"H-m! Suppose I learn that for myself! I'll start at the beginning. Your name is William Barker?"

"Yes. I told you that once."

"Where is your home? What city have you lived in mostly?"

The man hesitated.

"I was born in Gadsden, Alabama, if that's what you mean. Mostly I've lived in New York and around there."

"What cities around there?"

"Newark."

"Newark, New Jersey?"

"Yes. An' in Jersey City some, and Paterson, and a little while in Brooklyn."

"You met Mr. Warren where?"

"In New York. I was valet for a feller named Duckworth, and he went and died on me–typhoid; you c'n find out all about him if you want. Mr. Warren was a friend of Mr. Duckworth's, an' he offered me a job. We lived in New York for a while and then we come down here."

"How long ago?"

"'Bout four years–maybe five."

"What kind of a man was he–personally?"

Carroll watched his man closely without appearing to do so. He saw Barker flush slightly, and did not miss the jerky nervousness of his answer–that or the forced enthusiasm.

"Oh, I reckon he is all right. That is, he *was* all right. Real nice feller."

"You were fond of him?"

"I didn't say I was in love with him. I said he was a nice feller."

"Treated you well?"

"Oh, sure—he treated me fine."

"And yet he discharged you yesterday." Then Carroll bluffed. "Without notice!"

Barker looked up sharply. His face betrayed his surprise; showed clearly that Carroll's guess had scored.

"How'd you know that?"

"I knew it," returned Carroll. "That's sufficient."

Barker assumed a defensive attitude.

"Anyway," said he, "that didn't make me sore at him, because he give me a month's pay; and that's just as good as a notice, ain't it?"

"Ye-e-es, I guess it is." Carroll hesitated. "Did he pay you in cash?"

"Yeh—cash."

Again Carroll hesitated for a moment, while he lighted a cigarette. When he spoke again, his tone was merely conversational, almost casual.

"You've read the papers—all about Mr. Warren's murder, haven't you?"

"I'll say I have."

"What do you think about it?"

Again that startled look in Barker's eyes. Again the nervous twitching of hands.

"Whatcha mean, what do I think about it?"

"The woman in the taxicab—do you think she killed him?"

Barker drew a deep breath. One might have fancied that it was a sigh of relief.

"Oh, *her*? Sure! She's the person that killed him!"

"He knew a good many women?" suggested Carroll interrogatively. "He got along pretty well with them?"

"H-m!" William Barker nodded. "You said it then, Mr. Carroll. Mr. Warren—he was a bird with the women!"

8
CARROLL MAKES A MOVE

No slightest move of Warren's erstwhile valet–no twitching of facial muscles, no involuntary gesture of nervousness, however slight–escaped Carroll's attention; but with all his watchfulness, the boyish-looking investigator was unostentatious, almost retiring in his manner.

And this modest demeanor was having its effect on William Barker, just as Carroll had known it would have, and as Leverage had hoped. Eric Leverage had worked with Carroll before, and he had seen the man's personal charm, his sunny smile, his attitude of camaraderie, perform miracles. People had a way of talking freely to Carroll after he had chatted with them awhile, no matter how bitter the hostility surrounding their first meeting. Carroll was that way–he was a student of practical every-day psychology. He worked to one end–he endeavored to learn the mental reactions of everyone of his *dramatis persoae* toward the fact of the crime he happened to be investigating; that and, as nearly as possible, their feelings at the moment of the commission of the crime, no matter where they might have been.

"It doesn't matter what a suspect says," he had told Leverage once. "Some of them tell the truth and some of them lie. Often the truth sounds untrue, while the lies carry all the earmarks of honesty. It's a sheer guess on the part of any detective. What I want to know is how my man felt at the time the crime was committed–not where he was; and how he feels now about the whole thing."

"But the facts themselves are important," argued the practical chief of police.

"Granted! But when you have facts, you don't need a detective. I'd rather have a suspect talk freely and never tell the truth than have him be reticent and stick to a true story."

Leverage's reply had been expressive of his opinion of Carroll's almost uncanny ability.

"Sounds like damned nonsense," said he; "but it's never failed you yet. And even you couldn't get away with it if you lost that smile of yours!"

Right now he was witnessing the magic of Carroll's smile. He had seen the antagonism slowly melt from Barker's manner. The nervousness was still there, true; but it seemed tinged with an attitude which was part friendliness toward Carroll and part contempt for his powers. That, too, was an old story to Leverage. More than one criminal had tripped over the snag of underrating Carroll's ability.

Barker's last statement–"Warren, he was a bird with the women!"–was true. Leverage knew it was true. Carroll knew it was true. There was the ring of truth about it. It mattered not whether Barker had an iron of his own in the fire–it mattered not what else he said which was not true–the two detectives knew that they had extracted from him a fact, the relative importance of which would be established later.

Just at present, knowledge that the dead man had been somewhat of a philanderer seemed of considerable importance. For one thing, it established the theory that he had been planning an elopement with the woman in the taxicab. That being the case, a definite task was faced–first, find the woman; then find some man vitally affected by her elopement with Warren.

Carroll betrayed no particular interest in Barker's statement. Instead, he smiled genially, a sort of between-us-men smile, which did much to disarm Barker.

"A regular devil with 'em, eh, Barker?"

"You spoke a mouthful that time, Mr. Carroll! What he didn't know about women their own husbands couldn't tell him."

"Married ones?"

"Oh, sure! He was a specialist with them."

"Then most of this gossip we've been hearing has a basis of fact?"

A momentary return of caution showed in Barker's retort.

"I don't know just what you've been hearin'."

"A good many stories about his love affairs—with women who were prominent socially."

Barker shrugged.

"Most likely they're true; although it's a safe bet that a heap of 'em was lies. Men folks have a way of lyin' about women that way, even where they'll tell the truth about everything else. They've got women beaten ninety-seven ways gossiping about that sort of thing."

"You know a thing or two yourself, Barker?"

The man flushed with pleasure.

"Oh, I ain't nobody's pet jackass, when it comes to that!"

"Now you"—Carroll's tone was gentle, almost hypnotic—"of course you know who the woman is that Mr. Warren was planning to elope with?"

"I know—"

Suddenly Barker paused, and his face went white. He compressed his lips with an effort and choked back the words. Leverage, leaning forward in tense eagerness—knowing the verbal trap that Carroll had been planting—sighed with disappointment, and relaxed.

"Say, what the hell are you driving at!"

"Nothing." One would have sworn that Carroll was surprised at Barker's flare of anger—or else that it had passed unnoticed. "I just figured that you, having been his valet, and knowing a good deal about him, would have knowledge of this."

"He wasn't in the habit of discussin' his lady friends with me," growled the ex-valet surlily.

"Of course he wasn't; but you know, of course? You guessed?"

"No, I didn't do nothin' of the kind. Say, what are you tryin' to do–trip me up or somethin'?"

"Of course not. Why should I be interested in tripping you up?"

"You was sayin'–"

"Don't be foolish, Barker! It wouldn't do me a bit of good to–er–trip you up. All I want is whatever knowledge you have which may prove of interest in solving this case."

The man's eyes narrowed craftily.

"You ain't got no suspicions yourself, have you?"

"Suspicions of what?"

"Who that dame in the taxicab was."

Carroll laughed infectiously.

"Goodness, no! If I had, I wouldn't be seated here chatting with you."

Again the expression of relief flashed across Barker's face–a bit of play lost by neither detective. Carroll was toying idly with a gold pencil on the end of his waldemar. His outward calmness exasperated Leverage. From this point of the interview, the chief of police would have dropped the attitude of trustful friendliness and resorted to a little practical third-degree stuff. He was fairly quivering with eagerness to bluster about the room and extract information by main force.

And a hint of Leverage's mental seethe must have been communicated to Carroll, for the younger man turned the battery of his sunny gaze upon the chief of police and nodded reassuringly. The effect was instantaneous. Leverage's temporary resentment departed much as the gas escapes from a pin-punctured balloon. He gave ear to Barker's speech.

"N'r you ain't the only one who don't know who that woman was. *I* don't!"

"You knew he was planning to elope, though?"

The man shook his head doggedly.

"I knew he was leavin' the city for good, if that's what you mean."

"No-o, not exactly. I knew that much myself. What interests me is this—was he planning to leave with some woman?"

Barker hesitated before replying, and when he did answer it was patent that his words were chosen carefully.

"I don't hardly reckon he was, Mr. Carroll. Mind you, I'm not sayin' he wasn't; but then again I ain't sayin' he was. I can't do nothin' only guess—same as you can."

"I see!" Carroll was apparently unconscious of Barker's flagrant evasion. "What I don't understand is this—when Mr. Warren was publicly engaged to Miss Gresham, why did he try to elope with her?"

"Elope with Miss Gresham?" Barker paused; then a slow, calculating smile creased his lips. "Miss Gresham—her he was engaged to! Dog-gone if I don't believe you've hit the nail on the head, Mr. Carroll!"

"What nail?"

"About her bein' the woman in the taxi. You know some fellers is like that—they'd a heap rather elope with a woman they're crazy about than stand up in a church and get married. They're sort of romantic." Barker was waxing loquacious. "You know, you must be right. Fact, if you put it right up to me, I'd say there wasn't no doubt that Miss Gresham was the woman in the taxicab."

"I had that idea," responded Carroll slowly. "But what I can't understand, Barker, and what you might help me figure out, is this—why should Miss Gresham kill Mr. Warren?"

"Huh! Ask me somethin' easy, will you? I never was good at riddles."

Leverage marveled at the change in the two men. Apparently Carroll had swallowed hook, line, and sinker. Of course, Leverage was pretty sure that he had not; but he was also sure that Barker thought he had. And Barker was volunteering information—plenty of it—that was absolutely valueless. For the first time he was forcing the conversational pace, and Carroll seemed serenely content to drag limply along.

"Reckon she might have been jealous of him?" drawled Carroll.

"Jealous? Maybe. I ain't sayin' she wasn't. Of course, she must have heard a good many things about him and other women; and when a woman gets downright jealous there ain't much sayin' what she wouldn't do. Not that I'm sayin' Miss Gresham croaked him. I ain't sayin' nothin' positive; but if you're askin' me who he'd most naturally elope with, why I'd say it was the girl he was engaged to marry. If he wasn't going to marry her, what did he ever get engaged to her for?"

Carroll nodded.

"Certainly sounds reasonable." He paused, and then: "Where were you about midnight last night?"

"I was"–Barker's figure stiffened defensively, and his eyebrows drew down over the deep-set eyes–"I was just shootin' some pool."

"Shooting pool?"

"Un-huh!"

"Where?"

"At Kelly's place."

"Where is that?"

The man hesitated, flushed, and then, somewhat sullenly:

"On Cypress Street."

"That's pretty close to the Union Station, isn't it?"

"Not so close."

"About how far away?"

Again the momentary hesitation.

"'Bout a half-block."

"And you were shooting pool there?"

"Sure I was! I c'n prove it."

Carroll grinned disengagingly.

"You don't need to prove anything to me, Barker. And for goodness' sake get the idea out of your head that I'm suspecting you of anything. I had to talk matters over with you. You knew more about the dead man than anyone else; but I couldn't think you had anything to do with it, could I? You're not a woman!"

Barker grinned sheepishly.

"That's all right, Mr. Carroll. And as for me bein' a woman—well, you're sure a woman killed him, ain't you?"

"As sure as anyone can be. And now"—Carroll rose—"I'm tremendously obliged for all the information you've given me. Any time you run across anything more that you think might prove of interest, look me up, will you?"

"Sure! Sure!" Barker's tone was almost hearty. "You're a regular feller, Mr. Carroll—a regular feller!"

The two detectives departed. Carroll spoke to Cartwright as he passed:

"Keep both eyes on that fellow Barker," he ordered curtly. "I'll send Reed up to team with you. Don't let him get away. Nab him if he tries it."

Cartwright nodded briefly, and Carroll and Leverage climbed into the former's car. As they rounded the corner, Leverage turned wide eyes upon his professional associate.

"Carroll?"

"Yes?"

"You beat the Dutch!"

"How so?"

"You didn't swallow that bird's yarn, did you?"

"Of course not," answered Carroll calmly.

"I didn't think so; but you had me worried, with that innocent look of yours. Me, if I was wantin' to play safe on this case, I'd arrest William Barker *pronto*."

"Why?"

"Because," snapped Leverage positively, "I think he was mixed up in Warren's murder!"

"Aa-ah!" Carroll refused to become excited. "You do?"

"Yes, I do. What do you think?"

"I think this," answered Carroll. "I think that Mr. William Barker knows a great deal more about the case than he has told!"

9
ICE CREAM SODA

They drove in silence to headquarters, each man busy with his thoughts. It was not until they were alone in Leverage's sanctum that the subject of the recent interview was again broached. It was Leverage who brought it up, in his characteristically gruff way.

"I reckon you're wonderin', Carroll, about what I said back yonder in the car?"

"About arresting Barker?"

"Yes. I guess you're figuring what I'd arrest him for, eh?"

"I'm interested—yes."

"I'd arrest him for this." Leverage leaned forward earnestly, his attitude that of a man eager to convince. "Let's admit right off the reel that the skirt in the taxicab croaked Warren. Looks like she did, anyway; but whether she did or not, it's an even bet that there was a man mixed up in it somewhere. And if that man isn't Mr. William Barker, then I'll eat a month's pay."

"You're sure there was a man mixed up somewhere?"

"Certainly. This murder deal was planned in advance. It must have been. Things couldn't just work out that way. And no woman, no matter how much she wanted to bump Warren off, could think of a thing that complicated. Even if she did think of it, she wouldn't have the nerve to carry it out that way. Ain't I right?"

"You may not be right, Leverage; but you're certainly logical."

"Good! Now, so far, we ain't got any man in this case except Barker."

Carroll shook his head.

"You're wrong there."

"How?"

"Somewhere in this town is some man who is interested in the woman with whom Warren was planning to elope. Don't forget this, Leverage–I let Barker ramble on. I like to hear 'em talk. The minute he jumped at the idea that the woman in the taxi was Miss Gresham, I knew perfectly well that he knew she was not. I also believe that he knows who the woman was. Further, I believe that she is socially prominent. That being the case, it is a safe guess that there is some man who might commit a murder, provided he knew in advance of the elopement. Our task now is to discover that woman and, through her, the man interested."

Leverage frowned thoughtfully.

"Listens good," he volunteered at length. "Another thing–Barker admits he was shooting pool in Kelly's place last night around midnight; and Kelly's place is only half a block from the Union Station. That sounds significant!"

"It does; and then again it may mean nothing. What I am striving for is to make William Barker feel that he is safe. The safer he feels, the more readily he will talk. No matter how many lies he tells, everything that he says is of value. He didn't know, of course, that we already had a perfect alibi for Miss Gresham; but even if we hadn't, his assumed belief that she committed the crime would have assured me that she did not. No-o, I think we'd better not arrest the man unless he forces our hand–tries to jump town, or something like that. Better let him remain at large and talk frequently. If he has anything to betray, there's more chance that he'll do it that way. Don't you think I'm right?"

"I wouldn't admit it if I didn't, Carroll. I've seen you in action too often to believe you're ever wrong."

Carroll flushed boyishly.

"Don't be absurd, Leverage! I'm often wrong–very wrong. And don't think that I'm a transcendent detective; they don't really exist, you know. I'm merely trying to be human, to learn the nature of the people with whom I'm dealing. I try to learn 'em as well as they know themselves–maybe a little better; and then I try to separate the wheat of vital facts from the chaff of the inconsequential."

"Just the same," insisted Leverage loyally, "you always get 'em!"

"And when I do, it is because I have used nothing more than plain common sense. Don't think that I attach no importance to physical clues. They're immensely valuable; but the one weakness in a criminal is his lack of common sense. His perspective is awry, his sense of values distorted. Usually he bothers his head about a myriad minor details, and pays but scant attention to the genuinely important things. It is upon that weakness that I am banking–particularly so in the case of Barker."

"I insist that you're a wonder, Carroll!"

"And I insist that you're foolishly complimentary. Did you ever stop to realize, Eric, that when a crime is committed the advantage lies entirely with the detective? The detective can make a thousand mistakes during the course of his investigations and still trap his man; but the criminal cannot make one single error–not *one!*"

"Maybe so, David; but it takes a good man to recognize that one, and to know what to do with it."

Carroll grinned and left, and then for two days devoted himself to a study of the conditions surrounding the murder–that and routine matters. The trunk, for instance, was duly returned by the railroad from New York, and Carroll and his friend made a minute investigation of every article contained therein. Their search was well-nigh fruitless. The trunk contained little save the wardrobe of a well-dressed man–suits, shirts, underwear, shoes, caps. There were also golf and tennis togs; a few books; a handsome leather secretary, containing a good many personal letters and one or two business missives which were of little interest. Altogether the examination of the trunk–a process which occupied three hours–established nothing definite, save that there was nothing to be discovered. Its results were hopelessly negative.

Meanwhile the city sizzled with gossip of the Warren murder. The seemingly impenetrable mystery surrounding the case, its many sensational features, the admission of the police department that the woman in the case was not Hazel Gresham, fiancee of the dead man, yet the certainty that there was a woman, and that she was of the better class–all this served to keep the tongues of men and women alike wagging at both ends.

Carroll was besieged with anonymous letters. Dozens of prominent married women were mentioned as having been, at one time or another, the object of Warren's amorous attentions. Carroll read each one carefully and filed it away. He had hoped for this, but the results had far exceeded his expectations, and he found himself bewildered rather than assisted by the response from nameless individuals who were morbidly eager to be of help.

The detective knew that the running down of each individual trail–the investigation of each of Warren's supposed affairs of the heart–would be an interminable procedure. And so far not a single one of the letters had varied from another. They connected Warren's name with that of some married woman, and let it go at that. It was quite evident that the dead man had been very much of a Lothario; too much so for the mental ease of the investigator who was struggling to link the cause of his death with one particular affair.

The reporters allowed their imaginations to run wild. The story was what is known, in the parlance of the newspaper world, as a "space-eater." City editors turned their best men loose on it and devoted columns to conjecture. There was little definite information upon which to base the daily stories that were luridly hurled into type. Thus far Spike Walters, driver of taxicab No.

92,381, was the only person under arrest, and only those persons too lazy to exercise their minds were willing to believe that Spike was guilty or that he knew more of the crime than he had told.

Carroll read each news story attentively. No wild theory of a pop-eyed reporter, hungry for fact, was too absurd to receive his careful attention. But they proved of little assistance. With the spot-light of publicity blazing on the crime, the investigation seemed to have become static. There was no forward movement; nothing save that in the brain of David Carroll salient facts were being seized upon and meticulously catalogued for future reference.

Cartwright and Reed, the plain-clothes men detailed to shadow William Barker, reported nothing suspicious in that gentleman's movements. He seemed to be making no effort to secure employment, but, on the other hand, there was little of interest in what he did do. Again the stone wall of negative action.

Barker spent his mornings in his boarding-house, apparently luxuriating in long slumbers; he ate always at the same cheap restaurant; and his afternoons and evenings were devoted largely to the science of eight-ball pool at Kelly's place. There may have been significance in his loyalty to Kelly's place; but if there was, it was too vague for Carroll to consider. He merely remembered the fact that Barker was a steady patron of the pool-room near the Union Station, and filed it away with his other threads of information concerning the murder.

Carroll was frankly puzzled. The case differed widely from any other with which he had ever come in contact. Usually there was an array of persons upon whom suspicion could be justly thrown; a collection of suspects from whom the investigator could take his choice, or from whom he could extract facts which eventually might be used to corner the guilty person. In the present case there was no one to whom he could turn an accusing finger.

Of course, he was convinced that William Barker knew a great deal about the crime and the events which preceded it; but Barker wouldn't talk–and he, Carroll, had no evidence that enabled him to bluff, to draw Barker out against his will.

The crime seemed to have lost itself in the sleety cold of the December midnight upon which it was committed. The trails were not blind–there were simply no trails. The circumstances baffled explanation–a lone woman entering an empty taxicab; a run to a distant point in the city; the discovery of the woman's disappearance, and in her stead the sight of the dead body of a prominent society man–that, and the further blind information that the suit-case which the woman had carried was the property of the man whose body was huddled horribly in the taxicab.

The woman, whoever she was, had either been unusually clever or unusually lucky. Minute examination of the interior of the cab had revealed nothing–not a fingerprint, nor a scrap of handkerchief. There was absolutely nothing which could serve as a clue in establishing her identity.

And yet, somewhere in the city–a city of two hundred thousand souls–was the woman who could clear up the mystery.

Convinced that she was prominent socially, Carroll kept a close eye upon the departures of society women for other cities. His vigil had been unrewarded thus far. And the public as a whole waited eagerly for her apprehension, for the public was unanimous in the belief that the woman in the taxicab was the person who had ended Warren's life.

The very fact of having nothing definite upon which to work was getting on Carroll's usually equable nerves. He had little to say to Leverage regarding the case, for the simple reason that there was very little which could be said. Leverage, on his part, watched the detective with keen interest, sympathizing with him, and exhibiting implicit confidence, but the men didn't agree upon the correct procedure. Leverage was all for arresting Barker and charging him with the murder.

"You'll learn some facts then, Carroll," he insisted.

But Carroll shook his head.

"It wouldn't get us anywhere, Eric. We couldn't prove him guilty."

"No-o, but that don't make no difference. Of course the law says a man is innocent until you prove he ain't, but that ain't what the law does. If we arrest this here Mr. William Barker, everybody's going to believe he's guilty until he proves himself innocent."

"And you think he can't do that?"

"No! At least I'm gambling on this—Barker can't prove himself innocent without telling who is guilty!"

But Carroll refused to arrest the man. He knew that Leverage disapproved, but he also knew that Leverage was sportsman enough to let him handle the case in his own way.

On one of his long strolls through the downtown section of the city—daily walks which helped him to think connectedly—David Carroll felt a hand on his arm and heard an eager feminine voice in his ear:

"Gracious goodness! If it isn't the perfectly marvelous Mr. David Carroll!"

Carroll bowed instinctively. Then his lips expanded into the first wholesome smile he had experienced in forty-eight hours.

"Miss Evelyn Rogers!"

"You did recognize me, didn't you? How simply splendiferous! I'm awfully glad we met!"

"So am I, Miss Rogers."

She dropped her voice confidentially.

"Will you do me a *great* favor—an *enormous* favor?"

"Certainly. What is it?"

"It's this." She looked around carefully. "I told some of my friends that you are a friend of mine, and they don't believe it. They're over yonder in that ice-cream place. Now, what I want you to do for me is to show 'em. I want you to take me over there and buy me an ice-cream soda!"

Carroll laughed aloud as he took her by the arm and piloted her through the traffic. He asked only one question:

"What flavor?"

10
A DISCOVERY

If Evelyn Rogers, amply clad as to fur around the neck but somewhat under-dressed as to lace stockings about the legs, had desired to create a sensation among her friends, she more than succeeded. She preceded Carroll into the place, her eyes glowing pridefully, skirted the table at which her friends sat, then stopped abruptly, forcing Carroll to do likewise.

"Mr. Carroll," she said sweetly, "I want to introduce you to my friends." She called them by name. "Girls, this is Mr. Carroll, the famous detective!"

Carroll bowed in his most courtly manner, and assured them that he was delighted to make their acquaintance. He insisted that it was always a pleasure to meet any friends of his very dear friend, Miss Rogers. The girls at the table giggled with embarrassment, and one or two of them made rather pallid attempts at repartee. Then Carroll and the seventeen-year-old found a table in the very center of the floor, even as a boy, recognizing Carroll, appeared at their elbow.

The detective studied the list intently. Apparently there was no subject in the world more vital at that moment than the selection of just the proper concoction. Finally he looked up and shook his head.

"I can't decide," he announced gravely. "They all sound so good! Walnut banana sundae; strawberry glory; peach Melba; chocolate parfait, with whipped cream and cracked walnuts; elegantine fizz—Help me out, please."

She, too, plunged into the labyrinth of toothsome titles. Finally she emerged smiling.

"Have you ever tasted a chocolate fudge-sundae?"

"No-o, I'm afraid not."

"Well, it's just the *elegantest* thing–vanilla ice-cream with hot fudge poured over it, and as soon as they pour the fudge–it's steaming hot, you know–simply scalding–it forms into a sort of candy, and then when they serve it–"

"I fancy you want one, too, don't you?"

"Oh, goodness me, yes! I *always* eat chocolate fudge sundaes. They're simply scrumptious–but they do take the edge off one's dinner appetite. Personally, I don't care so very much. I believe we eat too much anyway, don't you, Mr. Carroll? I read in a book once that after you reach a certain point in eating–that is, after you've swallowed just the right number of calories–the rest don't do you a single particle of good. And besides, ice-cream is healthy, and certainly there's nothing with more nourishment in it than chocolate–unless it is raisins. I like raisins well enough–"

Carroll turned to the boy.

"Two chocolate fudge sundaes," he ordered; "and put a few raisins on one of them."

He found the large eyes of the girl turned upon him adoringly.

"Do you know," she said, "that when I said the other day that you were the most wonderful, the most marvelous man in the world, I didn't even know half how wonderful or marvelous you really were?"

"Thanks! And what caused the discovery?"

"The way you acted just now. Why, I'm sure those girls think that you've known me all your life–or that we're engaged, or something!"

Carroll was a trifle startled.

"Engaged?"

"Why not? You don't *look* like an old man."

The detective chuckled.

"Nor do I feel like one when I'm with you. You're deliciously refreshing."

"And you are–are–exquisite! Do you know, when I'm with you, I feel inspired to great deeds–to noble–er–attainments."

"Really?"

"Uh-huh! Honest to goodness. And did I really help you by what I told you the other day?"

"You certainly did, Miss Rogers. There isn't a doubt of it."

She lowered her voice and leaned confidentially across the table.

"Will you tell me something?"

"Surely?"

"Who really killed Mr. Warren?"

"Eh?"

"Who really did kill him?"

"Why, I'm sure I don't know. I'm trying to find out."

"Oh, pshaw! You can't pull the wool over *my* eyes! You couldn't have been working on the case this long and not have discovered the–the–malefactor."

"But that's exactly what I have done. Also it's why I rather hoped that you might have a little more information for me."

"Me? Information for you? How wonderful! As if you'd be interested in anything I might know! Although I'm not an absolute fool. Gerald says I am, of course–he's my brother-in-law–but then Gerald isn't anything but an old crab, anyway. Hateful thing! But *you* don't think I am, do you?"

"No, indeed. Ah, here we are!"

The chocolate fudge sundaes were served, and for a few moments they gave themselves over to the task of enjoying them. It was Evelyn who spoke first.

"What do you want me to tell you?"

"Almost anything. For instance–you knew Roland Warren pretty well, didn't you?"

"Oh, yes, indeed! I've known him forever and ever. He was an awfully nice boy, and crazy about me–simply wild! That is, he was before he died."

"H-m! And you saw a good deal of him?"

"Oceans! He used to call at the house all the time. It *was* funny, too. Gerald used to think he was the one Roland was coming to see, and Naomi—she's my sister—used to think that he was coming to see her; and all the time I knew that I was the person he was calling on. It's funny, isn't it, how old folks will get those queer ideas?"

"Your sister is so very old?"

"Terribly. She was thirty on her last birthday."

"Horrors! She *is* ancient, isn't she?"

"Awfully! Although Naomi isn't so bad looking—"

"*Your* sister couldn't be."

"Aw, quit kidding! But she isn't bad-looking, really. Lord knows she deserves a better husband than she drew. Honestly, when the divine providence was handing out shrubbery, they planted a lemon-tree in his yard just before he was born."

"Probably your sister doesn't agree with your opinion."

"Oh, yes, she does! Of course, she doesn't talk to me about it, but I know she ain't wild about Gerald. How could she be? He's old enough to be her father—forty-two, if he's a minute. Don't think of anything but business and making money. And he's *terribly* jealous!"

"A very complimentary picture you draw of him."

"If I wrote what I thought about him, I could be arrested for sending it through the mails. Goodness knows, no husband at all is a hundred per cent better than a man like that. Not that he beats Naomi. Fact is, I'd think he was more human if he did. Only time I ever like him is when he flies up in a rage. He swears simply *elegantly*!"

"Indeed?"

"I love it. And I don't think it's wicked to love swearing, do you? I was reading in a book once something about swearing being a perfectly natural mental reaction, or something—like a safety-valve on a steam-engine. If the engine didn't have the safety-valve, it would blow up. So if it's true that swearing is like that, then there can't be any harm in it; because anything that keeps a person from blowing up must be pretty good, don't you think?"

"It does sound reasonable."

"Not that I swear myself–not out loud, anyway, but sometimes, when I'm right peeved at Gerald or Naomi or somebody, I get in my room and say swear-words right out loud. And I feel ever so much better for it!"

The conversation languished while she again attacked the sundae. Carroll spoke:

"Have you seen your friend, Miss Gresham, lately?"

"Hazel? I'll say I have–although she's horribly weepy since poor Roland was killed. Of course, I'm not heartless or anything like that; but what's the use of crying all the time when there are just as good fish in the sea as ever were caught? I told her that, but it don't seem to do a single bit of good. She just keeps saying, 'Poor Roland is dead,' just as if I didn't know it as well as she does–him having been crazy about me even before he was about her. I'm sort of afraid it's gone to the poor girl's head. She's simply *horribly* upset!"

"That's not unnatural, is it?"

"No-o, I suppose not; but it's terribly old-fashioned."

"Does she–discuss the affair much?"

"All the time."

"What does she think about the woman in the taxicab?"

"You mean the woman who killed him?"

"Yes."

"Well!" positively. "If I was that woman, I'd hate to meet Hazel Gresham–if Hazel knew it!"

"But she has no suspicion of any certain person?"

"Goodness, no! How could she have? Of course, we agreed that it was some vampire; but we can't decide which one. Most of the women we know don't go in for killing men; and a heap of them are married, anyway."

"Anyway?"

"Yes. You wouldn't expect a nice chap like Roland to be eloping with a *married* woman, would you? Not in real life?"

Carroll with difficulty concealed a smile. The girl was a refreshing mixture of world-old wisdom and almost childish innocence. She was a type new to him, and, as such, absorbingly interesting.

"How about Miss Gresham's brother?" he inquired idly. "How does he take it?"

"Oh, Garry seems all upset, too; but then the more I talk to people, the more I think I'm the only level-headed one in the world. I haven't got a bit excited over it, have I?"

"Not a bit. And now"—Carroll rose and reached for the check—"suppose we go?"

"Where?" she asked naively.

The opening was too obvious.

"Where do you usually go with young gentlemen who meet you down-town in the afternoons?"

"Picture show," she answered frankly. "Wouldn't you just *adore* to see that picture at the Trianon to-day? They say it's *stupendous*!"

"Perhaps."

They walked up the street together. On the way they passed Eric Leverage. That gentleman bowed heavily and stood aside in surprise, while an exclamation, rather profane, issued from his lips. David Carroll and a seventeen-year-old girl headed for a picture show! The thing was unbelievable. Leverage shook his head sadly and passed on as Carroll and Evelyn disappeared behind the din of an orchestrion.

The picture proved not at all bad, although Evelyn excited adverse comment from spectators unfortunate enough to be sitting within range of her constant chatter. Apparently there was no stopping her. She talked and talked and talked.

The picture ended eventually, and they left the theater. Night had descended upon the city, and the busy thoroughfare was studded with thousands of lights, which glared coldly through the December chill. Principally because he did not know what else to do, Carroll requested permission to take her home in his car. She accepted with rather disarming alacrity.

Carroll had about run out of conversation, and his ears were tired by the incessant din of the girl's talk. He followed her directions mechanically, and eventually they rounded a corner in the heart of the city's best residential district. Evelyn designated a white house which stood back in a large yard.

"That's it," said she. "You'd better turn first, so you can park against the curb."

Carroll slowed down and swung around. He was tired of the loquacious girl, and anxious to be rid of her; but as he swung his car across the street on the turn, something happened which riveted his attention.

The door of Evelyn's home opened. A man and woman stood framed in the doorway. Then the door closed, and the man descended the steps, moved down the walk to the street, and strode swiftly away. For perhaps three seconds he had been held clearly in the glare of Carroll's headlights.

When the detective spoke, it was with an effort to control his tone, to make his question casual.

"Did you see that man, Miss Rogers?"

"Yes."

"Do you know him?"

"Goodness me, no! He's been here before, though."

Carroll stopped his car at the curb. He assisted Evelyn to the ground. Then he made a strange request.

"I wonder, Miss Rogers, whether you'd allow me to call on you some evening?"

Evelyn's eyes popped open with the marvel of it.

"You mean you want to come and call on *me*? Some *evening*?"

"If you will allow me."

"Allow you? Why, David Carroll–I think you're simply–simply–*grandiloquent*! When will you come?"

"If your sister will permit–"

"Bother Sis! To-morrow night?"

"Yes, to-morrow night."

She executed a few exuberant dance steps.

"Oh, what'll the girls say when I tell 'em?"

Carroll climbed thoughtfully back into his car. He saw Evelyn enter the house, but his thoughts were not with her. He was thinking of the man who had just left.

Carroll never forgot faces, and he had recognized the visitor.

The man was William Barker, former valet to Roland Warren!

11
LOOSE ENDS

Carroll's forehead was seamed with thought as he turned his car townward and sent it hurtling through the frosty air. He drove mechanically, scarcely knowing what he was doing.

He was frankly puzzled, enormously surprised and not a little startled. The afternoon had been at first amusing, then interesting–then utterly boring. Evelyn's chatter had put him in a state of mental coma–a lethargy from which he had been rudely aroused at sight of William Barker leaving the residence of Evelyn Rogers' sister.

There was something sinisterly significant in what he had seen. Not for a moment did he entertain the idea that Barker had been seeking employment. Negativing that possibility was the cold statement of the disinterested young girl that Barker had been there before, and, too, the fact that Barker was leaving from the front door instead of through the servant's door.

Obviously, then, Barker's mission had little to do with the matter of domestic employment. And now that he had stumbled upon something tangible–something definite– certain salient facts which had come to him through the haze of girlish chatter began to stand out and assume proper significance.

For instance there was her constant repetition of the fact that Roland Warren had been a frequent visitor at the Lawrence home. That might mean nothing: it might mean a great deal. Certainly it was indicative of a close friendship between the dead man and the members of that household. He paid little heed to the girl's protestations that Warren had been in love with her. No expert in the ways of the rising generation, Carroll yet knew that no man of Warren's maturity had unleashed his affections on a girl who yet lacked several years of womanhood. The dead man had been too much of an epicure in femininity for such as that.

But Carroll knew that in that house there was another woman: Naomi Lawrence—Evelyn's sister. And while Evelyn had dismissed the sister with a few words, Carroll remembered that the girl had described her as being "not so bad looking" and had also said that Mrs. Lawrence fancied that when Warren called at the house, he was calling on her.

There, too, was the matter of Gerald Lawrence to be considered. Evelyn insisted that Gerald was "an old crab" and also that he was of an exceedingly jealous disposition. If that were true, then his jealousy, coupled with a possible intimacy between Mrs. Lawrence and Warren might have been ample motive for the taxicab tragedy.

It was all rather puzzling. Carroll's mind leaped nimbly from one mental trail to another. He held himself in check, afraid that his deductions were proceeding too swiftly. He was acutely conscious of the danger of jumping too avidly on this single tangible clue which had come to him after four days of fruitless search. There was danger, and he knew it, of attaching untoward importance to a combination of circumstances which under other conditions might not have excited him in the slightest degree.

It was there that the case bewildered him—and he was not slow in confessing his bewilderment. Up to this moment there had been an appalling dearth of physical clues—of things upon which a line of investigation could be intelligently based. And he knew that now something had turned up, he must watch himself lest the circumstance assume unreasonable and unwarranted proportions.

The somber outline of police headquarters bulked in the night. Carroll swung down the alley, shut off his

motor and entered. He found Leverage in his office and
settled at once to a discussion of developments. But when
he would have spoken Leverage cut him off. Leverage had
news–and Leverage was frankly proud of the fact that he
had news.

"Just got an interesting report from Cartwright," he
announced.

"Regarding Barker?" Carroll hitched his chair forward
eagerly.

"Yes."

"What is it?"

"Yesterday afternoon at five o'clock William Barker
went to the residence of Mr. and Mrs. Gerald Lawrence.
He was in the house eighteen minutes."

"Why wasn't this told me last night?"

"Cartwright didn't think anything of it. He included it
in his report which was turned in to me this morning."

"Why did he think it was unimportant?"

"Said he thought Barker was probably looking for a
job."

"And he doesn't think so now?"

"No-o. That is: he thinks circumstances make an
investigation worthwhile. You see, just a few minutes ago
Barker went to the Lawrence home again. This time he
was there four minutes."

"Does Cartwright know who was at home at that
time?"

"He thinks so. He says a maid let Barker in and that
apparently Mrs. Lawrence let him out. A young girl–
whom Cartwright believes to be Mrs. Lawrence's sister–
drove up just as Barker was leaving. She was in the car
with some man–but he didn't get out. Then, just a minute
ago, Gerald Lawrence reached home. So the idea is that
Mrs. Lawrence was alone with the servants when Barker
called."

"And yet he only remained four minutes?"

"That's what Cartwright 'phoned." Leverage paused. "What do you make of it, Carroll?"

"Off-hand," answered the youthful-appearing detective, "I'd say that Barker had called to see *Mr.* Lawrence."

"Why?"

"We'll suppose Lawrence was home on the occasion of Barker's first visit–do you know whether he was?"

"No. I asked. Cartwright doesn't know. Couldn't stay, you know–because he was under orders to follow Barker. Tonight he sent Reed after Barker and he watched the Lawrence house."

"Good. If it is so that Lawrence was at home when Barker called yesterday evening and Barker then remained eighteen minutes; whereas this afternoon, when we know that no one but Mrs. Lawrence was there– and he remained but four minutes–it is fairly reasonable to suppose that he was calling to see Mr. Lawrence."

"I think you're right, Carroll."

"I'm not at all convinced about that. But if we're proceeding along lines of pure logic, that is the answer."

"How about the man who drove up with the kid sister?"

Carroll smiled. "I'm sure he had nothing whatever to do with the murder."

"Good Lord! I didn't think he had. But still he may have been a friend, and–"

"That man was all right. I know that."

"You *know*?" Leverage was incredulous.

"Yes." Carroll grinned. "I was the man!"

"You–? Holy sufferin' mackerel! Sa-a-ay! Was that chicken I seen you with downtown, Lawrence's sister-in-law?"

"Yes. Miss Evelyn Rogers. And Good Lord! Leverage, how that girl can talk! She holds all records for conversational distance and speed. She talked me dumb."

Leverage was staring respectfully at Carroll. "If you were the man who was with her, David—you must have seen Barker when he left the house."

"I did."

The face of the chief showed his disappointment: "That's what I get for thinking I had a real surprise up my sleeve. You sit back with that innocent kid face of yours and let me spill all the dope—and then tell me perfectly matter-of-factly that you knew it all the time. How'd you ever get wise to the thing, anyway?"

Carroll was honest. "No thanks to my sagacity, Leverage. One of those pieces of bull luck which I have always contended play an enormous part in solving crime. In the first place Evelyn Rogers came to me the day after Warren was killed to assure me that Miss Gresham had a perfect alibi. This afternoon she lassoed me and dragged me into an ice cream place because she wanted to prove to some of her school companions that we were really friends." Carroll chuckled. "I quaffed freely from the fountain of youth—and enjoyed it awhile. Then I got bored stiff. Took her to the movies—she invited me—and did it only because I've passed beyond the years of adolescence and didn't know how to crawfish out of it. After which—because it seemed the proper thing to do—I volunteered to ride her home in my car. And it was then that I saw Barker leaving the Lawrence home. So you see, Leverage, my knowledge is the result of pure accident—and not at all the fruit of keen perception."

"Well, anyway—Carroll: you knew! And that takes the edge off what I told you."

"Not at all," returned Carroll seriously. "For while what I discovered is perhaps valuable—that combined with the fact that Barker has been there once before: and that on his first visit when Lawrence was probably at home he stayed nearly five times as long as he did when we know that Lawrence was not there—that is of help—or ought to be."

"What do you think of it?"

Carroll hesitated. "I don't know what to think, Eric. I'm afraid I'm thinking about it more than I have any right. We've been so long without anything to work on, that we're liable to let this bit of information throw us off our balance. But of course we'll look more deeply into it."

"How?"

Again Carroll chuckled. "Our little friend, Miss Rogers, is suffering from a large case of hero-worship. I'm it! And so—when I saw Barker leaving her home—I immediately made an engagement to call upon her to-morrow night!"

"*You* call on that kid—" Suddenly Leverage lay back in his swivel chair and gave vent to a peal of raucous laughter. He banged his fist on the arm of the chair: "Oh! *Boy*! That's the snappiest yet. David Carroll paying a social call on a seventeen-year-old kid! Mama! Ain't that the richest—"

Carroll made a wry face. "Needn't rub it in. It's bad enough anyway. And"—growing serious—"I'm hoping to meet Mr. and Mrs. Lawrence. They ought to prove interesting."

But Leverage could not tear himself away from the sheer humor of the situation: "What the devil you and her going to talk about? Foxtrot steps? Is the camel walk vulgar? Frat dance? Next week's basketball game? Sa-a-ay! David—I'd give my chances of Heaven to be hidden behind the door."

"So would I," said Carroll wryly.

"Above all things," counseled Leverage with mock severity: "Don't you go making love to her."

Carroll reached a muscular hand across the table. His sinewy fingers closed around a glass paperweight. He held this poised steadily. "One more crack out of you, Eric, and I'll slam this against your head. You're a pretty good chief of police—but you're a rotten humorist."

"Just the same," grinned the chief, "I can see that this joke is on you! And now—what?"

"For one thing," and Carroll's manner was all business again, "I want every bit of dope I can get on Gerald Lawrence and his wife. I know that Warren was very intimate at the house: friendly with both wife and husband, according to what Miss Rogers says. That connects them up. What I want to find out now is where both of 'em were the night Warren was killed. Put a couple of your best men out to gather this dope—there isn't any of it too minor to interest me. Meanwhile, I'll pump the kid. I have a hunch that this isn't going to be a cold trail."

"It better not be—or Mr. David Carroll is going to find himself with one unsolved case on his hands. Yes, sir—if this is a blind lead, we're up against it for fair."

"It isn't going to be entirely blind," postulated Carroll. "Barker assures us of that!"

12
A Challenge

At four o'clock the following afternoon Carroll received from Chief Leverage a detailed report on Gerald Lawrence:

"He's a manufacturer," said Leverage. "President of the Capitol City Woolen Mills. Rated about a hundred thousand—maybe a little more. He's on the Board of Directors of the Second National. Has the reputation of being hard, fearless—and considerable of a grouch. Age forty-two.

"Married Naomi Rogers about five years ago. She was twenty-five then—thirty now. Supposed to be beautiful—and would be a society light except that Lawrence doesn't care for the soup-and-fish stuff. Report has it that they're not very happy together. His parents and hers all dead. Evelyn, her kid sister, lives with them.

"They employ a cook and two maids. No man-servant at all. Roland Warren was pretty intimate at the house, but so far as I can discover there was no scandal linking the names of Warren and Mrs. Lawrence. Of course, him knowing her pretty intimately and being friendly at the house, you could probably find a good many folks who would say nasty things. But there hasn't been the real gossip about her and him that there was about a heap of other women in this town.

"Warren and Lawrence were pretty good friends. Warren was a stockholder in the woolen mills. On the other hand it seems as though Warren was at the house a good deal more than just ordinary friendship would have indicated. But that's just an idea. And there's your dope—"

"And on the night of the murder?" questioned Carroll. "Where were they?"

"Mrs. Lawrence was at home. Lawrence—if you're thinking of him in connection with it—seems to have an iron-clad alibi. He went to Nashville on a business trip and didn't get back until the following morning."

"Alibi, eh?" Carroll's eyes narrowed speculatively, "are you *sure* he was in Nashville all that time?"

"Hm-m!" Leverage shook his head. "I don't know—but I can find out."

Carroll rose. "Do it please. And get the dope straight."

Carroll went to his apartment where he reluctantly commenced dressing for the ordeal of the night. He felt himself rather ridiculous—a man of his age calling on a girl not yet out of high school. The thing was funny—of course—but just at the moment the joke was too entirely on him for the full measure of amusement.

At that, he dressed carefully, selecting a new gray suit, a white jersey-silk shirt and a blue necktie for the occasion. At six-thirty Freda served his dinner and at fifteen minutes after eight o'clock he rang the bell of the Lawrence home.

The door was opened by Evelyn: palpitant with excitement, and garbed attractively in the demi-toilette of very-young-ladyhood.

"Mr. Carroll—so good of you to come. I'm simply tickled to death. Let me have your hat and coat. Come right into the living room—I want you to meet my brother-in-law and my sister—"

Sheepishly, Carroll followed the girl into the room. Mr. and Mrs. Lawrence rose politely to greet him.

At the sight of the man he had really come to see, Carroll was conscious of an instinctive dislike. Lawrence was of medium height, slightly stooped and not unpleasing to the eye. But his brows were inclined to lower and the eyes themselves were set too closely together. He was dressed plainly—almost harshly, and he stared at Carroll in a manner bordering on the hostile.

The detective acknowledged the introduction and then turned his gaze upon the woman of the family. There he met with a surprise as pleasant as his first glance at Lawrence had been unpleasant.

There was no gainsaying the fact that Naomi Lawrence was a beautiful woman. Dressed simply for an evening at home in a strikingly plain gown of a rich black material, and with her magnificent neck and shoulders rising above the midnight hue—she caused a spontaneous thrill of masculine admiration to surge through the ordinarily immune visitor in the gray suit.

Her face was almost classic in its contour: her coloring a rich brunette, her hair blue-black. No jewelry, save an engagement ring, adorned her perfect beauty, and Carroll felt a loathing at the idea that this magnificent creature was the wife of the stoop-shouldered, sour-faced man who stood scowling by the living room table.

He gravely acknowledged the introduction of the young lady upon whom he had called: feeling a faint sense of amusement at Lawrence's overt disdain—and a considerable embarrassment under Naomi's questioning, level gaze. For a few moments they talked casually—but that did not satisfy Evelyn, and she dragged him into the parlor—

"—just the eleganest jazz piece—" Carroll heard as through a haze "—just got it—feet can't keep still—play it for you—"

He found himself standing by the piano, the door between the music room and the living room unaccountably closed. Evelyn banging out the opening measures of the "elegant jazz piece."

He was still staring moodily at the closed door when the din ceased and he again heard Evelyn's voice. "A penny for your thoughts, Mr. Carroll. A real honest-to-goodness-spendable penny!"

"I was thinking," he remarked quietly, "that your sister is a very beautiful woman."

"Naomi? Shucks! She isn't bad looking—but she's *old*. Abominably old! Thirty!"

He glanced down on the girl and smiled. "That does seem old to you, doesn't it?"

"Treacherously! I don't know what I'd ever do if I was to get that old. Take up crocheting, probably."

The conversation died of dry-rot. Carroll was not at all pleased. His excuse–the plea that he had come to call upon Evelyn–had been taken too literally. He had fancied–in his blithe ignorance of the seventeen-year-old ladies of the present day–that he could engineer himself into a worthwhile conversation with the Lawrences. Since meeting them, he was doubly anxious. There was a thinly veiled hostility about the man which demanded investigation. And about the woman there was a subtle atmosphere of tragedy which appealed to the masculine protectiveness which surged strong in his bachelor breast.

But Carroll was a sportsman. The girl had carried things her own way–and he was too game to spoil her evening. Therefore, he temporarily gave over all thought of a chat with the Lawrences and devoted himself to her amusement. He informed her that the jazz music she had strummed was simply "glorious" and that he regretted he knew very little popular stuff. She leaped upon his remark–

"Oh! Do *you* play: *really*?"

He was in again. "I have–a little."

"I wonder if you would? Here's the *grandest* little old song I bought downtown–" and she placed on the piano a gaudy thing with the modest title–"All Babies Need Daddies to Kiss 'Em." Its cover exposed a tender love scene wherein a gentleman in evening clothes was engaged in an act of violent osculation with a young lady whose dress was as short as her modesty. Carroll shrugged, placed his long, slender fingers on the keys– shook his head–and went to it.

He played! A genuine artist–he tried to enter into the spirit of the thing and succeeded admirably. The itchy syncopation rocked the room. His hostess snapped her fingers deliciously and executed a few movements of a dance which Carroll had heard referred to vaguely as the shimmy. In the midst of the revelry he gave thought to Eric Leverage and chuckled.

He played the chorus a second time–then stopped on a crashing chord. Evelyn's face was beaming–

"Gracious! You can play, can't you?"

"I used to–Suppose we talk awhile."

She agreed–reluctantly. They seated themselves in easy chairs before the gas logs. Evelyn glanced hopefully at the chandelier. "I wish the belt would slip at the power house, don't you?"

"Why?" innocently.

"Oh! Just because Bright lights are such a nuisance when a girl has a feller calling on her. And these logs give a perfectly respectable light, don't they?"

"Indeed they do–but perhaps we'd better leave the others on."

She sighed resignedly. "I guess we'd better. Sis is so darned proper and Gerald is an old crab–they might say something."

"I suppose they might. By the way, didn't they think it was–er–strange: my coming to see you tonight?"

She turned red. "Suppose they did–what difference does that make? I'm not a child and if a gentleman wants to call on me I guess they haven't got any kick."

"What did they say when you told them I was coming?"

"They didn't believe me at first. Then Sis said you were too old–and you're not old at all–and Gerald said–he said–" she giggled.

"What did Gerald say?"

"He said, 'Damned impertinence!'"

"H'm-m! I wonder just what he meant?"

"Oh! Goodness! It doesn't matter what Gerald means. He makes me weary. He's simply *impossible*–and I can't see what Sis ever married him for."

"I suppose she saw more in him than you do. They must be very happy together."

"Happy? Poof! Happy as two dead sardines in a can. They can't get out—so they might as well be happy. Besides, he's away a good deal."

"He is, eh? When was his last out-of-town trip?"

Carroll was interested now—he had steered the conversation back to matters of importance: "Oh! 'bout four days ago—you know—the day dear Roland was killed by that vampire in the taxicab."

"He was away that night: all night?"

"Uh-huh! All night long. And would you believe that Sis—who is scared of her shadow at night—was the one who suggested that I go spend the night with Hazel? And it's certainly fortunate she did, because if she hadn't I wouldn't have been with Hazel all night and you awful detectives would probably not have believed her story that she was at home in bed, and then you would have arrested her for murdering Roland—and she'd have gone to jail and been hanged—or something. Wouldn't she?"

"Hardly that bad. But it was fortunate that you were there. It made the establishing of the alibi a very simple matter. And you say your sister—Mrs. Lawrence—is nervous at night?"

"Oh! Fearfully. She's just like all women—scared of rats, scared of the dark, scared of being alone—perfectly disgusting, I call it."

"Quite a few women are that way, though—"

"I'm not. I'm scared of snakes and flying bugs and things like that. But I don't get scared of the dark—pff! Who's going to hurt you? That's what I always say. I believe in figuring things out, don't you I read in a book once where—"

"But maybe you do Mrs. Lawrence an injustice. Maybe she isn't as afraid at night as you imagine."

"She is, too."

"Yet you say she let you spend the night at Miss Gresham's house when Mr. Lawrence was out of the city and there wasn't anybody on the place but the servants—"

"Worse than that: the servants don't even live on the place. She spent the night here all alone—!"

"Then all I'll say is that she is a brave woman. When did Mr. Lawrence get back from Nashville?"

"Oh! Not until ten o'clock the following morning. And believe me, he was all excited when he read about Roland in the papers. Poor Roland! If you were only a girl, Mr. Carroll—you'd know how terrible it is to have a man who's crazy about you and engaged to your best friend and everything—go and get himself murdered. Why, when I read the papers that morning, I couldn't hardly believe my own eyes. I just said to myself 'it can't be!' I said it over and over again just like that. Having faith, I think they call it. I was reading in a book once about having faith—"

She talked interminably. Carroll ceased to hear the plangent voice. He was thinking of what she had just told him—thinking earnestly. He knew he was desperately anxious to have a talk with the Lawrences, to talk things over in a casual manner. And tonight was his opportunity. He knew he'd never have another like it. He didn't want to be forced to seek them out in his capacity of detective.

From somewhere in the rear of the house he heard the clamor of a doorbell, then the sound of footsteps in the hall, the opening and closing of the front door—and then Naomi Lawrence appeared in the music room. Carroll could have sworn that her eyes were twinkling with amusement as she addressed Evelyn—pointedly ignoring him.

"Evelyn—that Somerville boy is here."

"Oh! Bother! What's he doin' here?"

"He says he came to call. He's got a box of candy."

"Piffle! What do I care about candy? He's just a kid!"

Naomi went to the hall door. "Right this way, Charley." And as the slender, overdressed young gentleman of nineteen entered the room, Carroll again glimpsed the light of amusement in Naomi's eyes.

Mr. Charley Somerville expressed himself as being "Pleaset'meetcha" and tried to conceal his vast admiration when Evelyn informed him that this was *the* David Carroll. Charley was impressed but he was not particular about showing it–Charley fancying himself considerable of a cosmopolite, thanks to a year at Yale. His dignity was excruciatingly funny to Carroll as the very young man seated himself, crossed one elongated and unbelievably skinny leg over the other and arranged the creases so that they were in the very middle.

"A-a-ah! Taking a vacation from your work on the Warren murder case, I presume?"

Carroll nodded. "Yes–for awhile."

"Detective work must be a terrible bore–mustn't it?"

"Sometimes," answered Carroll significantly.

"Charley Somerville!" Evelyn flamed to the defense of her friend's profession. "At least Mr. Carroll ain't–isn't–a college freshman."

"I'm a sophomore," asserted Charley languidly. "Passed all of my exams."

"Anyway," snapped Evelyn, "he ain't any kid!"

For a time the atmosphere was strained. Then Carroll recalled a particularly good college joke he knew and he told it well. After which Evelyn explained to Charley that Mr. Carroll was the wonderfulest piano player in the world and David Carroll, detective, strummed out several popular airs while the youngsters danced.

Horrible as the situation was, it appealed irresistibly to his sense of humor. He found himself almost enjoying it. And he worked carefully. Eventually his patience was rewarded. He succeeded in getting them together on a lounge with a photograph album between them. And then, very quietly and positively, and with a brief–

"Excuse me for a moment," he walked through the hall and into the living room.

Lawrence and his wife were at opposite sides of the library table. At sight of Carroll, Lawrence laid down his paper and rose to his feet.

"Well?" he inquired inhospitably.

Carroll laughed lightly. "It got too much for me. Too much youth. I dropped in here for a chat with you folks."

"I didn't understand that you had come to call on us," said Lawrence coldly.

"Why, I didn't–"

"You did!" snapped Lawrence. "I'm no fool, Carroll. From the minute I heard you were coming, I knew what you had up your sleeve. You wanted to talk about the Warren case! Now suppose you go ahead and talk–then get out!"

13
NO ALIBI

Carroll was rarely thrown from a mental balance, but this was one of the exceptions to a rule of conduct where poise was essential. His eyes half-closed in their clash with the coldly antagonistic orbs of his host. His instinctive dislike of the man flamed into open anger and he controlled himself with an effort.

One thing Lawrence had done: he had stripped from Carroll his disguise as a casual caller and settled down ominously to brass tacks. Carroll shrugged, forced a smile—then glanced at Naomi Lawrence.

She had risen and was staring at her husband with wide-eyed indignation. Undoubtedly she was horrified at his brusqueness. For the first time, she, too, had made it plain that Carroll was not welcome—that his ruse of calling upon Evelyn had been seen through plainly—but he could see that even under those circumstances she was not forgetful that he was a guest in her home and, as such, he was entitled to ordinary courtesy.

Carroll was more than a little sorry for her, and also a bit rueful at his own plight. Things had gone wrong for him from the commencement of the evening. And this—well, the gage of battle had been flung in his face and he was no man to refuse the challenge. But his muscles were taut until the soft voice of Naomi broke in on the pregnant stillness—

"Won't you be seated, Mr. Carroll?"

Carroll smiled gratefully at her. With her words the unpleasant tension had lightened. He dropped into an arm chair. Lawrence followed suit, his close-set eyes focused belligerently on Carroll's face, the hostility of his manner being akin to a personal menace. Naomi stood by the table, eyes shifting from one to the other.

"I'd rather," she suggested softly, "that we did not discuss the Warren case."

"It doesn't matter what you prefer," snapped her husband coldly. "Carroll forced himself upon us for that purpose—with a lack of decency which one might have expected. Let him have his say."

Carroll gazed squarely at Lawrence. "I'm sorry," he said, "that you see fit to act as you are doing."

"I asked for no criticism of my conduct."

"Just the same, dear—" started Naomi, when her husband interrupted angrily—

"Nor any apologies to him from you, Naomi. Carroll has placed himself beyond the pale by what he has done in having the impertinence to foist himself upon us as a social equal. Now, Carroll—are you ready with your little catechism?"

"Yes." The detective's voice was quite calm. "I'm quite ready."

"Well—ask." Lawrence paused. "You *did* come here to inquire about Warren, didn't you?"

Carroll could not forbear a dig: "I trust that you are not putting it upon me to deny your statement to that effect."

"I don't give a damn what you deny or affirm."

"Good! Then we know all about each other, don't we. You know that I am a detective in search of information and I know absolutely what you are!" That dart went home—Lawrence squirmed. "So I'll come right to the point. Is it not a fact that you were in this city at the hour Roland Warren is supposed to have been killed?"

He heard a surprised gasp from Naomi and saw that her face had blanched and that she was leaning forward with eyes wide and hands clutching the arms of the chair in which she had seated herself.

Lawrence leered. "As the kids would say, Carroll—that's for me to know and for you—super-detective that you are—to find out."

Carroll was more at ease now. Lawrence's sneering aggressiveness brought him into his own element and he was hitting straight from the shoulder: refusing pointblank to mince matters.

"I fancy I can," he returned calmly. "And now: is it not a fact that you despised Warren even though you pretended to be his friend?"

"That, too, is my business, Carroll. Do you think I'm going to feed pap to you?"

Carroll reflected carefully for a moment. Then suddenly his voice crackled across the room—"You know, of course, that you are suspected of Warren's murder?"

Silence! Then a forced, sickly grin creased Lawrence's lips—but his figure slumped, almost cringed. From Naomi came a choked gasp—

"Mr. Carroll! Not Gerald—"

Carroll paid no heed to the woman. He sat back in his chair, eyes never for one moment leaving Lawrence's pallid face. Nor did Carroll speak again—he waited. It was Lawrence who broke the silence—

"Is—this—what you—detectives—call the third degree?"

"It is not. Now get this straight, Lawrence—I came here to find out what you know about Warren and the circumstances surrounding his death. I wanted to be decent about the thing—to cause you no embarrassment if I was convinced that you were unconnected with the crime. You have forced my hand. You have driven me to methods which I abhor—"

"You haven't a thing on me," said Lawrence and his tone had degenerated into a half whine. "You can't scare me a little bit. I've got an alibi—"

"Certainly you have. So, too, have a good many men who have eventually been proven guilty."

Lawrence rose nervously and paced the room. "You asked me a little while ago if I was in this city at the hour when the crime was committed. I answered that it was for me to know and you to find out. I'll answer direct now–just to stop this absurd suspicion which has been directed against me: I was *not* in the city at that hour–or within six hours of midnight. I was in Nashville."

"At what hotel?"

"At the–" Lawrence paused. "Matter of fact, I wasn't at any hotel."

"You had registered at the Hermitage, hadn't you?"

"Yes, but–"

"When did you check out?" Carroll's voice was snapping out with staccato insistence.

"About four o'clock in the afternoon."

"Where did you go? Where did you spend the night?"

Lawrence shook his head helplessly. "I'll be honest, Carroll–I took several drinks–"

"Alone?"

"Yes. And at two o'clock in the morning when my train left I was at the station. I don't know what I did in the meantime–I don't remember anything much about anything."

"In other words," said Carroll coldly, "You have no alibi except your own word. On the other hand we know that you checked out of the Hermitage Hotel in Nashville at four o'clock. You could have caught the 4:25 train and reached this city at ten minutes after eleven o'clock. You have not the slightest proof that you didn't."

"I–I came down on the train which left there a little after two in the morning."

"Prove it."

There was a hunted look about Lawrence. "I can't prove it–a man can't prove that he came on a certain train–"

"Was there nobody on board who knew you?"

"I–don't know. I was feeling badly when I got in–the berths were all made up–I went right to sleep and when the porter woke me we were in the yards. I dressed and came right home."

"And yet–" Carroll was merciless "–you have no substantiation for your statements." He switched his line of attack suddenly: "What made you think I was coming here to discuss Roland Warren's death?"

It was plain that Lawrence did not want to answer– yet there was something in Carroll's mesmeric eyes which wrung words unwillingly from his lips–

"Just logic," he answered weakly. "I knew that you weren't calling to see Evelyn because you were interested in her. You knew Warren had been pretty friendly in this house–so you came to talk to us about it. Isn't that reasonable?"

"I don't believe I am here to answer questions, Mr. Lawrence. You invited me to ask them."

Naomi broke in, her voice choked with hysteria– "What are you leading to, Mr. Carroll? It is absurd to think that Gerald had anything to do with Mr. Warren's death."

Carroll swung on her, biting off his words shortly: "Do you *know* that he didn't?"

"Yes–I–"

"I didn't ask what you thought, Mrs. Lawrence. I am asking what you *know*!"

"But if he was in Nashville–"

"If he was, then he's safe. But he himself cannot prove that he was. And I tell you frankly that the police will investigate his movements very carefully. It strikes me as exceedingly peculiar that he checked out from the Hermitage Hotel at four o'clock in the afternoon when he intended taking a two a.m. train. Remember, I am accusing your husband of nothing. Our conversation could have been pleasant–he refused to allow it to be so. He classified me as a professional detective and put me on that basis in his home. I have merely accepted his invitation to act as one. If I appear discourteous, kindly recall that it was none of my doing."

"I'm sorry, Carroll," said Lawrence pleadingly. "I didn't know–"

"Of course you didn't know how much I knew–or might guess. You saw fit to insult me–"

"I've apologized."

"Your apologies come a trifle late, Lawrence. Entirely too late. Our relations from now on are those of detective and suspect–"

Again the flare of hate in Lawrence's manner: "I don't have to prove an alibi, Carroll. You have to prove my connection with the thing. And you can't do it!"

"Why not?"

"Because I was in Nashville at that time. And while perhaps I can't prove I was there–you certainly cannot prove I was not."

"That remains to be seen. Meanwhile, I'd advise you to establish that fact if you can possibly do so. And by the way: are you in the habit of indulging in these solitary debauches in neighboring cities?"

Lawrence flushed. "Sometimes. I used to be a heavy drinker, and–"

"Is that a fact, Mrs. Lawrence?"

"Yes," she answered eagerly: almost too eagerly Carroll thought–"he has had escapades like this–several times."

"And you are sure that his story is true?"

"Yes. Of course I'm sure. Why should he kill Mr. Warren? There isn't any reason in the world–"

"For your sake and his, I hope not. But meanwhile–"

"Surely, Mr. Carroll–you don't intend publishing what he has told you–about his drinking–alone–in Nashville?"

Carroll smiled. "No indeed. In the first place, I am not at all sure that he has told me the truth. In the second place, if I were sure of it–his alibi would be established and I have no desire whatever to injure a man because of a personal weakness."

Lawrence stared at Carroll peculiarly. "You mean that if I can prove the truth of my story, nothing will be made public about my–the affair–in Nashville?"

"Absolutely. Because you have treated me discourteously, Lawrence–I don't consider myself justified in injuring your reputation. I am after the person or persons responsible for the death of Roland Warren. Your intimate weaknesses have no interest to either me or the public."

Lawrence was silent for awhile, and then–"You're damned white, Carroll. The apologies I extended a moment ago–I repeat. And this time I'm sincere."

"And this time they are accepted."

"Meanwhile–you are welcome here whenever you wish to call. Perhaps–by talking to me–you yourself may establish the alibi which I know I have, but cannot prove."

Carroll rose and bowed. "Thank you. And now–I'll go. If you will express my regrets to Miss Rogers–"

Naomi accompanied him to the door. She extended her hand–"You're wrong, Mr. Carroll", she murmured. "Quite wrong!"

"You are sure?"

"I *know*! I really believe his story."

"I hope to–soon. But just now, Mrs. Lawrence–" He saw tears in her fine eyes. "You have nothing to fear from me if he is innocent."

She pressed his hand gratefully, and then closed the door. Carroll, inhaling the bracing air of the winter night, proceeded briskly to the curb. Then, standing with one foot on the running board of his car, he stared peculiarly at the big white house standing starkly in the moonlight–

"I wonder," he mused softly–"I wonder–"

14
THE SUIT-CASE AGAIN

Carroll drove direct to his apartments, despite his original intention of dropping by headquarters for a chat with Leverage. He wanted to be alone—to think—

The evening had borne fruit beyond his wildest imaginings. Fact had piled upon fact with bewildering rapidity. As yet he had been unable to sort them in his mind, to catalogue each properly, to test for proper value.

He reached his apartment and found it warm and comfortable. He donned lounging robe and slippers which the thoughtful Freda had left out for him, settled himself in an easy chair, lighted a fire which he kept always ready in the grate and turned out the lights. Then, with his cigar glowing and great clouds of rich smoke filling the air—he sank into a revelry of thinking.

Certain disclosures of the evening stood out with startling clarity. Chief among them was the inevitable belief that Gerald Lawrence had either killed Roland Warren or else knew who had done so—and how it was done. Yet Carroll tried not to allow his thoughts and personal prejudices to run away with him. He knew that now, of all times, he must keep a tight grip on himself.

Great as was the dislike which he had conceived for Lawrence—an instinctive repugnance which still obtained—he was grimly determined that he would not be swayed by his emotions. Therefore he deliberately reviewed Lawrence's story in the light of its possible truth.

Lawrence claimed that he belonged to that none too rare class of prominent citizens who once every so often respond to the call of the wild within them by going to a nearby city where they are not known and giving themselves over to the dubious delights of a spree. Publication of this fact alone would prove sufficient to injure Lawrence socially and in the commercial world. The old case of the Spartan lad–Carroll reflected. The disgrace lay in being discovered.

Also, it was perfectly plain to Carroll that at the outset of his conversation Lawrence had been smugly satisfied that he was possessed of a perfect alibi. It was only under Carroll's merciless grilling that he had been brought abruptly to realization that he had no alibi whatever. The same logic applied there, as in Leverage's theory that Barker's arrest would be an excellent strategic move. All Carroll had to do now was to arrest Lawrence for Warren's murder–and the burden of proof would have been shifted from the shoulders of the detective to that of the suspect. It would then devolve upon Lawrence to prove an alibi that Carroll knew perfectly well he could not prove–save by merest accident.

But that was a procedure which Carroll abhorred. Those were police department methods: wholesale arrests in the hope of somewhere in the net trapping the prey. Such a course was at the bottom–and Carroll knew it–of an enormous number of convictions of innocent men. And Carroll had no desire to injure Lawrence provided Lawrence was free of guilt in this particular instance. He didn't like the man–in fact his feelings toward him amounted to a positive aversion. But through it all he tried to be fair-minded–and he could not quite rid himself of the picture of Naomi Lawrence–Carroll was far from impervious to the appeal of a beautiful woman.

So much for the probable truth of Lawrence's story. The reverse side of the picture presented an entirely different set of facts. There was not alone the strange procedure of checking out of the big hotel at four o'clock in the afternoon when he intended catching an early morning train: but there was the information so innocently dropped by the loquacious Evelyn Rogers regarding Naomi's actions on the night of the murder.

According to Evelyn, her sister was an intensely nervous woman: one who stood in fear of being alone at night. And yet this sister had volunteered the suggestion that Evelyn spend the night with Hazel Gresham when her husband was supposed to be out of the city.

Carroll, well versed in applied psychology, knew that in such a combination of facts there lay an important clue. He was well satisfied that Naomi Lawrence had been satisfied that she was not to be alone that night!

Arguing with himself from that premise, the conclusion was inevitable: she knew that her husband would return from Nashville at midnight. She did not wish anyone—even Evelyn, to learn that he had done so. Therefore she got Evelyn out of the house!

The conclusion developed a further train of reasoning—one which Carroll did not at all relish, but which he faced with frank honesty. If he was right in his argument—then Naomi Lawrence had known of the murder before it was committed!

He shrank from the idea, but it would not down. He was not ready to admit its truth—but there was no denying its logic. There was something inexpressibly repugnant in the thought. He infinitely preferred to believe that Naomi hated her husband—was miserable with him—he preferred that to the idea that they were accomplices in the murder of a prominent young man.

Then, too, there were the strange visits of William Barker, former valet to Warren, to the home of the Lawrences. There was no doubt remaining in Carroll's mind that Barker knew a very great deal about Warren's murder. That being the case it was fairly well established that he was cognizant of the Lawrences' connection with the crime.

Carroll had started off with the idea that someone, in addition to the woman in the taxi-cab, had been instrumental in ending Warren's life.

Here, following a casual line of investigation, he had uncovered the tracks of two men, both of whom he was convinced knew more about it than they had cared to tell.

Both men—Barker and Lawrence—had acted peculiarly under the grilling of the detective. The former had been surly and non-informative, only to leap eagerly upon the first verbal trend which tended to throw suspicion upon a person whom Carroll knew—and whom Carroll knew Barker knew—was innocent. Gerald Lawrence, on the other hand, had been downright antagonistic until he made the startling discovery that his supposed alibi was no alibi at all—at which his attitude changed from open hostility to something closely akin to suppliance.

Then, too, there was the danger of injuring an innocent man because of his inability to prove an alibi. If Lawrence's story was true, it was perfectly natural that even in a condition of intoxication he would maintain his instinct for concealment of a personal weakness. The chances were then that no one had seen him either in Nashville—after the four o'clock train had left, or on the two a.m. train homeward bound.

Matters could not right themselves in Carroll's mind. He knew one thing, however—Evelyn Rogers was a wellspring of vital information. The very fact that she talked inconsequentialities incessantly—and occasionally let drop remarks of vital import—made her the more valuable. He knew that he had not seen the last of the seventeen-year-old girl. And he felt a consuming eagerness to be with her again, for now he had a definite line of investigation to pursue.

He slept soundly that night, and the following morning dropped in on Leverage. The Chief of Police had a little information—with all of which Carroll was already familiar. He told Carroll that Lawrence had been in Nashville and that he had checked out of the Hermitage hotel in time to catch the four o'clock train on the afternoon preceding the murder. Carroll satisfied Leverage by accepting it as information, made sure that nothing else of importance had developed, requested Leverage to ask the Nashville police to determine whether Lawrence had been seen in Nashville after 4:30 p.m.–if necessary to send one of his own men there–and left headquarters.

He made his way directly to a public telephone booth. He telephoned the Lawrence home and asked for Evelyn Rogers. A maid answered and informed him that Evelyn had left home fifteen minutes previously.

"Any idea where she was going?" questioned Carroll.

The answer came promptly: it mentioned the city's leading department store–"she's gone there to get a beauty treatment," vouchsafed the maid.

Carroll was not a little chagrined. Evelyn Rogers had put him in more hopeless positions in their brief acquaintanceship than he had experienced in years. There was his call upon her the previous night with its role of dual entertainer to the young lady with a nineteen-year-old college freshman. And now a vigil outside a beauty parlor.

But he went grimly to work. He located the beauty parlor on the third floor of the giant store, and paced determinedly back and forth before its doors.

A half hour passed; an hour–two hours. He concluded that Evelyn must be purchasing her beauty in job lots. When two hours and thirty-five minutes had elapsed Evelyn emerged–and Carroll groaned. With her were three other girls, as chattery, as immature, as Evelyn herself.

She swept down upon him in force–tongue wagging at both ends–

"You naughty, *naughty* man!" she chided. "You abso*lutely* deserted me last night. Why, I didn't even know that you had gone–until Sis came in and said you had asked her to extend your respects. Good gracious! I almost *died*!"

"I'm sorry–really," returned Carroll humbly–"But you seemed so interested in that young man–and I had gotten into an absorbing conversation with your sister and brother-in-law. I'm not used to girls, you know."

"Kidder! I think you're simply elegant!" She turned to her giggling friends and introduced them gushingly. Carroll was in misery–a martyr to the cause. But Evelyn would not let him get away. Through her sudden friendship with the great detective, Evelyn was building up a reputation that was destined to survive for years, and she was not one to fail to make the most of her opportunities.

It was not until almost an hour later, when the other three girls had left for their homes–left only after they had hung around until the ultimate moment before lunch–that Carroll found himself alone with his little gold mine of data. He bent his head hopefully–

"Were you planning to eat lunch downtown?"

She nodded. "Uh-huh!"

"Suppose we eat together?"

"Scrumptious!" There was no hint of hesitation in her manner. "I've been hoping ever since we met that you'd ask me."

They found a table mercifully secluded in the corner of the main dining room of the city's leading hotel. For once Carroll felt gratitude for the notoriously slow service. He begged her to order–and she did: ordered a meal which contained T.N.T. possibilities for acute indigestion. Carroll smiled and let her have her way–he was amused at her valiant efforts to appear the blasé society woman.

"I really did enjoy our conversation last night, Miss Rogers."

"Oh! Piffle! I don't fall for that."

"I did."

"Then why did you beat it so quick?"

"Well, you see–I suppose I was jealous of your elegantly dressed young friend."

"Him? He's just a kid. A mere *child*!"

"He seemed very much at home."

"Kids like him always do. They make me sick–always putting on as though they were grown up."

She secured an olive and bit into it with a relish. "Awful good–these olives. I love queen olives, don't you. I used to be crazy about ripe olives, but I read in a book once that sometimes they poison you, and when they do–there just simply isn't any anecdote in the world that can save you. So I figured there wasn't any use taking chances–"

Carroll let her run on until the meal was served. And it was then when she was satisfying a normal youthful appetite that he drove straight to the subject which had led to this masculine martyrdom.

"The day before Mr. Warren died," he said mildly–"are you sure that your sister made the suggestion that you spend the night with Miss Gresham?"

"Her? Sure she did."

"Didn't it strike you as peculiar–knowing that she'd be in the house alone all that night?"

"I'll say it did. I asked her was she nutty and she scolded me for being slangy. So I told her I should worry–if she wanted to suffer alone, and I went with Hazel. And it's an awful good thing I did, because if I hadn't she would have been arrested and tried and convicted and hanged–or something, and–"

"Oh! Hardly that bad. You're sure your sister was alone in the house that night?"

"Sure. Who could have been there with her?"

"I'm not answering riddles. I'm asking them."

"I've got my fingers crossed. The answer is that there wasn't anyone there. At first I thought she was going out–but she wasn't, and when I asked her was she, she got real peeved at me."

"Aa-a-h! You thought she was going out that night?"

"Uh-huh," came the answer between bites at a huge lobster salad.

"What made you think that?"

"Oh! Just something. You know, I don't get credit for having eyes, but I sure have. And I never did understand that business anyway. But then Sis always has been the queerest thing–ever since she married Gerald. Say–" she looked up eagerly–"ain't he the darndest old crab you ever saw in your life?"

"Why, I–"

"Ain't he? Honest?"

"He's not exactly jovial."

"He's a lemon! Just a plain juicy lemon. And I think she was a nut for marrying him."

"But–" Carroll proceeded cautiously–"you made the remark just now that something was the queerest thing. What did you mean by that?"

"Oh! I guess I was crazy–or something. But she got sore at me when I asked her–"

"Who?"

"Sis."

"What did you ask her?"

"Why–" she looked up innocently–"about that suit-case!"

"What suit-case? When was it?"

"It was the day before Mr. Warren died–I always remember everything now by that date. Anyway–I went in her room that morning to ask something about what I should take to Hazel's–and what do you think she was doing?"

"I'll bite," he answered with assumed jocularity–"what was she doing?"

"Packing a suit-case!"

"No?" Carroll was keenly interested–struggling not to show it.

"Yes, sir. I asked her what was she doing it for–and that's when she got peeved. I told you she was a queer one."

"Indeed she must be. Packing a suit-case—"

"And that ain't all that was funny about that, either, Mr. Carroll."

"No? What else about it was peculiar?"

"That suit-case—" and Evelyn lowered her voice to an impressive whisper—"was gone from the house the next day—and the day after it showed up again and when I asked Sis wasn't that funny she told me to mind my own business!"

15

A Talk With Hazel Gresham

Carroll tried to appear disinterested–strove to make his manner casual; jocular even. Evelyn was piecing the threads of circumstances together and the events surrounding the Warren murder were slowly clarifying in Carroll's brain.

But he knew that now, of all times, he must keep her from thinking that he had any particular interest in her chatter. She was completely off guard–and he knew that for his own interests, she must remain so.

So he assumed a bantering attitude–he resorted to what she would have termed "kidding."

"Aren't you the observant young woman, though? Not a single thing escapes your eagle eye, does it?"

She pouted. "Oh! Rag me if you want to. But I am *terribly* noticing. There ain't many things that happen which I don't get wise to."

"Not even vanishing suit-cases, eh?"

"No: not even that. It was funny about that, though. At first I thought maybe Sis was packing up to go meet Gerald in Nashville–but I figured out that it was bad enough to have to live with him here without chasing all over the country after him."

"You say that suit-case left the house after she packed it?"

"Sure pop."

"Who took it?"

"I don't know. Sis was out a couple of times that day–so I guess she did."

Carroll shrugged. "She was probably sending some of Mr. Lawrence's belongings to him in Nashville."

"Huh! There're some things even a great detective like you don't know. Don't you suppose I noticed that the clothes she was packing in that suit-case were *hers*?"

"Really?"

"You bet your life, I noticed. You see," she grew suddenly confidential. "There's a certain kind of perfume Sis uses–awful expensive. Roland Warren used to bring it to her. Well, I've been using it too–and Sis never did get wise. I only used it when she did–and when she smelled it, she didn't know that she was smelling what I had on. Well, it isn't likely she was sending that to Gerald, is it?"

"Hardly. But are you sure she packed it?"

"I'll say I am. I saw her do it. And then two days later I saw the bottle on her dressing table again–and so I just naturally looked to see if the suit-case was back and it surely was."

"But perhaps it never left the house?"

"Guess again, Mr. Carroll. I know–because just before I went to Hazel's I hunted all over for it, to get some of that extract myself. And the suit-case wasn't there. Believe me–it's *some* perfume, too!"

"You say Mr. Warren gave it to her?"

"He sure did. That man wasn't any piker, believe me. It costs twelve dollars an *ounce*!"

"No?"

"Yeh–goodness knows how much a pound would cost. I used it all the time–I knew when he gave it to Sis he meant it for me–because, like I told you, he was simply crazy about me. Told me so dozens of times. Said he came to see me. It used to bore him terribly when he'd have to sit in the room and talk to Sis and Gerald."

"I fancy it did–" Carroll summoned a waiter–"A little baked Alaska for dessert?"

"Baked Alaska! Oh! Boy! You sure spoke a mouthful that time. I'm simply *insane* over it!"

She evidently had not exaggerated. She absorbed enough of the dessert to have satisfied two growing men. It did Carroll good to witness her frank enjoyment of his luncheon. She glanced at her wrist watch and rose hastily—

"Goodness me, I've simply *got* to be going."

"Where?"

She made a wry face: "Hazel Gresham's. Honestly, women get queer when they grow up—get older than twenty. Hazel has been acting so *peculiarly* lately—"

"That's natural, isn't it, Miss Rogers? Her fiancé killed—"

"Oh! Shucks! I don't mean that. That wouldn't be queer. But there's something else bothering her. And when I try to get her to tell me what it is, she gets right snippy and tells me to mind my own business. And I'll tell you right now, Mr. Carroll—if there's one person in the whole world who always minds their own business—and who doesn't pay the slightest attention to other peoples' affairs—that person is me. I started that a long time ago when I read something someone wrote in a book about how much happier folks could be if they never bothered with other folk's business—and it struck me as awfully logical. And so that's what I've always done. Don't you think I'm sensible?"

"I certainly do. Very sensible. And I'm sorry Miss Gresham isn't feeling well."

"Oh! She feels well enough. She's just acting nutty. And as for when your name is mentioned—O-o-oh!"

"*My* name?" Carroll was genuinely surprised.

"Yes siree-bob! I started telling her all about what good friends you and I have gotten to be—and would you believe it! She jumped all over me—just like Sis did when I told her—and said I shouldn't associate with professional detectives—and it was immoral—and all that sort of thing."

"Indeed?"

"You bet she did. It was scandalous! Of course I told her what a ducky you are—but she begged me not to go with you anymore. I told her she was crazy—because I really don't think there's anything so very terrible about you—do you?"

"At least," smiled Carroll, "I won't eat you. But what you tell me about Miss Gresham is interesting. Why in the world should she be prejudiced against the man who is trying to locate the slayer of her fiancé?"

"Ask me something easy. I reckon it's just like I said before: when a woman grows up—gets to be twenty—she gets mentally unbalanced—or something. Honestly, I haven't met a woman over nineteen years of age in the *longest* time who didn't have a crazy streak in her somewhere. Have you?"

"I'd hardly say that much—" They had crossed the hotel lobby, swung through the doors and were standing on the sidewalk unconsciously braced against the biting wind which shrieked around the corner and cut to the bone, giving the lie to the bright sunshine and its promise of warmth.

"Brrrr!" shivered Evelyn—and Carroll rose eagerly to the hint.

"I'd be delighted to ride you to Miss Gresham's in my car—"

"Would you? That'd be simply splendiferous! And I'd like Hazel to meet you—then she'd know that you're just a regular human being in spite of what everyone says."

During the drive to the Gresham home, which stood on the side of the mountain at the extreme southern end of the city—Evelyn did about a hundred and one per cent of the talking. She blithely discussed everything from the economic effect of the recent election to the campaign against one-piece bathing suits for women: indicating well-defined, if immature opinions on every subject. She informed him that she was delighted with suffrage and opposed to prohibition, that the League of Nations would be all right if only it was not so far away, that she was sincerely of the belief that straight lines would pass out within the year and the girl with the curvy figure have a chance again in the world, that fur coats were all the rage–and he ought to see her sister's–it was the *grandest* in the city, that–she orated at length on any subject which occurred to her tireless mind; securing his dumb Okeh to her views–and liking him more and more with each passing minute because he treated her seriously: like a full grown woman of twenty–or something.

They pulled up at the curb of the Gresham home. As they did so Garry Gresham swung out of the gate, paused–and his eyes widened in astonishment at sight of Carroll. Then he stepped quickly to the curb as Carroll and the girl alighted.

"Hello, Garry," greeted Evelyn boldly. It was the first time she had ever called him by his first name. But Gresham did not notice. He nodded a curt "Hello, Evelyn" and addressed himself to Carroll–eyes level, manner direct.

"What do you want here, Carroll?"

There was an undertone of earnestness in the young man's words which the detective did not miss. He simulated innocence: "I? Nothing–"

Garry Gresham frowned. "You had no particular reason for coming here?"

"None whatever. Why?"

"I fancied it was peculiar–after your original suspicion of my sister–"

Carroll laughed good-naturedly. "Rid your mind of that, my friend. I merely happened to be downtown with Miss Rogers–and drove her up here in my car. As a matter of fact, if you have no objection, I'd like very much to meet your sister."

"Why?"

"Because she was Roland Warren's fiancée. Because she can tell me some things about Warren which no one else can tell me. Because the Warren case is almost as far from solution as it was one minute after the killing occurred."

Gresham thought intensively for a moment. "You can give me your word of honor, Carroll, that you are convinced that my sister is not connected in any way with the crime?"

"I can, Gresham. So far as I now know, your sister has no connection whatever with the case. But she must necessarily be in possession of certain personal details regarding Warren which I'd like to find out."

Gresham started back toward the house. "You may talk to her," he decided briefly—"if she is willing. But I prefer to be present during the interview."

Carroll bowed. "As you will, Gresham."

They walked to the house and Garry led the way to the front hall. Evelyn, considerably piqued at being ignored, took advantage of his disappearance in search of his sister, to open up a broadside of inconsequential chatter before which her previous efforts paled into insignificance. And it was in the midst of her verbal barrage that Gresham appeared at the far end of the hall with his sister.

Carroll was pleasantly surprised. Evelyn's protestations of intimacy with Hazel Gresham had implanted in his mind the impression that she was decidedly of the flapper type. He was glad to find that she was not.

She was not a beautiful girl: rather she belonged in that very desirable category which is labeled "Sweet." There was an attractive wistfulness about her—an undeniable charm, a wholesomeness—the sort of a woman, reflected Carroll instantly, whom a sensible man marries.

There was no hint of affectation about her. Her eyes were a trifle red and swollen and she seemed in the grip of something more than mere excitement. But in her dress there was no ostentation—it was somber, but not black. And she came straight to Carroll—her eyes meeting his squarely—and they mutually acknowledged Evelyn's gushing, but unheard, introduction—

"Miss Gresham—"

"Mr. Carroll–"

They seated themselves about a small table which stood in the center of the reception hall, and even Evelyn sensed the undercurrent of tenseness in the air. Her tongue became reluctantly still although she did break in once with a triumphant–"Ain't he like I told you he was?" to Hazel.

It was Garry who introduced the subject. "Mr. Carroll wants to ask you something about Roland," he said softly–and Carroll, intercepting the look which passed between brother and sister, felt a sense of warmth–a pleasant glow; albeit it was tinged with guilt–as though he had blundered in on something sacred.

The girl's voice came softly in reply: her gaze unwavering.

"What is it you wish to know, Mr. Carroll?"

The detective was momentarily at a loss. He conscripted his entire store of tact–"I don't want to cause you any embarrassment, Miss Gresham–"

"This is no time for equivocation, Mr. Carroll. You may ask me whatever you wish."

"Thank you," he answered gratefully. "You have, of course, heard that there is a woman connected with Mr. Warren's death–the woman in the taxicab."

Her face grew pallid, but she nodded. "Yes. Of course."

He watched her closely–"Have you the slightest idea–the vaguest suspicion–of that woman's identity?"

"No!" she answered–and he knew that she had spoken the truth.

"You have thought of it–of her–a good deal?"

"Naturally."

"Mind you–I'm not asking if you *know*–I'm merely asking if you have a suspicion."

"I have not–not the faintest."

"You were quite satisfied–pardon the intense personal trend of my questions, Miss Gresham–that during his engagement to you, Mr. Warren was–well, that he was carrying on no affair with another woman?"

"I say, Carroll–" It was Garry Gresham who interrupted and his voice was harsh. But his sister halted him with a little affectionate gesture–

"Mr. Carroll is right, Garry: he must know these things." She turned again to Carroll. "No, Mr. Carroll–I knew of no such affair–nor did I suspect one. When I became engaged to Mr. Warren I placed my trust in him as a gentleman. I still believe in him."

"Yet we *know* that there *was* a woman in that cab!"

"No-o. We know that the taxi-driver *says* there was."

"That's true–"

Hazel Gresham leaned forward: her manner that of a suppliant. "Mr. Carroll–why don't you abandon this horrible investigation? Why aren't you content to let matters rest where they are?"

"I couldn't do that, Miss Gresham."

"Why not?"

"Mr. Warren's murderer is still at large–and as a matter of duty–"

"Duty to whom? I am content to let the matter rest where it is. All of your investigation isn't going to restore Roland to life. You can only cause more misery, more suffering, more heartbreak–"

"It is a duty to the State, Miss Gresham. And, frankly, I cannot understand your attitude–"

"She has had enough–" broke in Garry Gresham. "She's been through hell since–that night."

"I'm afraid, though–"

"Mr. Carroll–you *can* call it off, if you will." Hazel Gresham rose and paced the room. "The case is in your hands. You can gain nothing by finding the person who committed the–the–deed. Let's drop it. Do me that favor, won't you? Let's consider the whole thing at an end!"

David Carroll was puzzled. But he was honest–"I'm afraid I cannot, Miss Gresham. I must, at least, try to solve it."

She paused before him: figure tensed–
"Then let me say, Mr. Carroll–that I hope you fail!"

16
THE WOMAN IN THE TAXI

From the Gresham home, David Carroll went straight to headquarters. Developments had been tumbling over each other so fast that he found himself unable to sort them properly. He wanted to talk the thing over with someone, to place each new lead in the investigation under the microscope in an attempt to discern its true value in relation to the killing of Roland Warren.

Eric Leverage was the one man to whom he could talk. And, locked in the Chief's office, he told all that he knew about the case, detailing conversations, explaining the situation as he understood it, reserving his suspicions and watching keenly for the reaction on the stolid mind of the plodding, practical Chief.

Carroll placed an exceedingly high valuation on Leverage's opinion—even though the minds of the two men were as far apart as the poles. But Leverage was a magnificent man for the office he held: competent, methodical, intensely orthodox—but typical of the modern police in contradistinction to the modern detective.

Carroll knew that modern police methods have received a great deal more than their share of unjust criticism. He knew that the entire theory of national policing is based on an exhaustive system of records and statistics. It operates by brute force and all-pervading power rather than by any attempt at sublety or keen deduction. The former is so much safer as a method. And the combination of the two—keen analysis, logical deduction and plodding investigation—can perform wonders, which explains why Carroll and Leverage worked hand-in-hand with implicit confidence in one another.

Leverage listened with rapt attention to the report of his friend. Occasionally the corners of his large humorous mouth twitched as Carroll touched on one or two of the lighter phases of his investigation–and once Leverage even twitted him about becoming "one of these here butterfly investigators"–but Carroll knew that no word of his escaped the retentive brain of the chief of the city's police force, and that each was being carefully catalogued with truer knowledge of its proper importance than Carroll had yet been able to determine.

"And so," finished Carroll, "there you are. The thing is in as pretty a mess as I care to encounter. Frankly, I don't know which way to turn next–which is why I wanted to talk things over. Perhaps, between us, we can arrive at some solution of the affair–determine upon some course of action."

"Yes," responded Leverage slowly, "perhaps we can. Only trouble is–there are so many different ways of spillin' the beans that we're takin' a chance no matter what we do. Answer me this, David: if you had to point out one person right now as the guilty one–which'd you choose?"

Carroll shook his head. "You know I don't like to answer questions of that sort."

"But you can tell me–"

"No-o. It might start your mind working along lines parallel to mine–and I prefer to have you buck me. But, in perfect honesty, I'll tell you that I'm all at sea. I couldn't conscientiously make an arrest now."

"Well–I'm willing to air my opinions," volunteered the Chief. "And I'm telling you that if it was up to me to make an arrest to-day I'd nab Mr. Gerald Lawrence–and haul in William Barker for good measure."

"M-m-m!" Carroll nodded approvingly. "Sounds reasonable. How about the woman?"

"That's what's got me puzzled. I've worked on that end of it, and I've had several of my best men circulating around trying to gather dope from the gossip shops–but there doesn't seem to be a clue from this end. Anyway–I don't believe Warren was killed by the woman in the taxi!"

Carroll was genuinely impressed. "You don't?"

"No. Don't believe any woman–I don't care who–would have killed him under those circumstances."

"You mean you believe the woman in the taxi had nothing to do with it?"

"I don't mean anything of the kind. I know darn well she had something to do with it–but I don't believe she did the actual killing. That's why I'd arrest this bird Lawrence and also William Barker. They either killed the man or they know all about it."

"But," suggested Carroll slowly, "suppose we admit that your theory is correct–and I've thought of it myself: how and where was that body put into the taxicab?"

Leverage shrugged: "That's where you come in, Carroll. I ain't the sort of thinker who can puzzle out something like that. Of course I'd say the only place the shift could have been made was when the taxi stopped at the R. L. & T. railroad crossing–and every time I think that it strikes me I must be wrong. Because any birds working a case like that couldn't have counted on such a break in luck."

"It might have been," suggested Carroll, "that two men entered the cab at that crossing: Warren and another–both alive, and the killing might have occurred between then and the time the cab reached number 981 East End Avenue."

"Might have–yes. But something tells me it didn't. It's asking too much–"

"Then what *do* you think happened?"

"I don't think. There just simply isn't anything you can think about an affair like that. You either know everything or you don't know a thing!"

"I think you're about right, Leverage. And now—let's run over the list we have in front of us. Spike Walters—the taxi driver—comes first. What about him?"

Leverage rubbed his chin. "Funny about Spike, Carroll—I think the kid's story is true."

"So do I."

"But unless there's some other answer to this affair—it's damned hard to believe that the body could have been dumped into that cab, or that the killing could have occurred there, without Spike knowing about it. Ain't that a fact?"

"It is."

"And if he knows anything he hasn't told, the odds are on him to know a whale of a sight more. And if he knows a whole heap—then the chances are he knows enough to justify us in keeping him in jail."

"You're right, Leverage. If Spike is innocent he's not undergoing any enormous hardship. But if his story is untrue in any particular—then it is probably entirely false. And since we cannot understand how that body got into the cab or where the murderer went—we've got to hold on to Spike. Meanwhile, we both believe him."

"You said it, David. Now, next on the list we have Barker. What about him?"

"I don't like Barker particularly," said Carroll frankly. "He hasn't what you would call an engaging personality. Not only that, but we are agreed that he knows a great deal about the case which he hasn't told—and doesn't intend to tell unless we force him to it. But we'll go back to him later: he's too important a link in the chain to pass over casually when we're trying to hit on a definite course of action. Remembering, of course, that his visits to the Lawrence home have a certain degree of significance."

Leverage chuckled grimly. "You're coming around to my way of thinking, David Carroll. Remember, I wanted to stick that bird behind the bars the first day we talked to him—when we first knew he was lying to us."

"Yes–but we wouldn't have gained anything–then. Perhaps now the time is ripe to try some of that third degree stuff. But let's take up the others. My little friend, Miss Evelyn Rogers, for instance."

Leverage chuckled. "Go to it, David. You know more about that kid than I ever will–or want to. Ain't suspecting her of being the woman in the taxi, are you?"

"Good Lord! No! She hasn't that much on her mind. And if we manage to solve this case, we can thank her. That little tongue of hers wags at both ends–and out of the welter of words that drip from her lips–I've managed to extract more information than from every other source we've tapped. I've been awfully lucky there–"

"Don't talk like a simp, David–'tain't luck. That's your way of working. And because there isn't anything flashy about it–you call it luck. Why, you poor fish–there isn't any other man in the country who'd have had the common sense to do what you did–to know that it would be a sensible move."

"Some day, Eric," grinned Carroll, "I'm going to throw you down–I'm going to flunk on a case. And then you'll say to my face what you must often have thought–that I'm a lucky, old-maidish detective."

"G'wan wid ye! Fishing for compliments–that's what you are."

Carroll grew serious again. "I think we're safe in eliminating Evelyn Rogers from our calculations except as a gold mine of information. Which takes us to her friend–Hazel Gresham."

"And Garry Gresham. You say he didn't want you to discuss the case with his sister."

"They both acted mighty peculiarly," agreed Carroll. "One of them, I'm sure, knows something about that case–has some inside dope on it. And the one who knew has told the other one–the affection between them is something pretty to look at, Leverage."

"You think one of them is in on the know?"

"Yes, I think so. And I think that their information touches someone pretty close to them. That's obviously why they pleaded so hard with me to call off the investigation."

"M-m-m—They're pretty good friends to the Lawrences, aren't they!"

"Yes—with Naomi Lawrence, anyway. I don't believe Gerald Lawrence is especially friendly with anyone. But the Greshams and Mrs. Lawrence are pretty intimate."

"And you believe that the alibi Miss Rogers established for Hazel Gresham is good?"

Carroll hesitated a moment before replying. When he did speak it was with obvious reluctance: "I hate to say so, Leverage—because I like Evelyn Rogers and I took an instant liking to both Hazel Gresham and her brother. But there seems to be something wrong about it. I do think that Evelyn Rogers believed she was telling the truth—but I'm not so sure that her dope was accurate. Just where the inaccuracy comes—I haven't the least idea—but I'm not letting my likes and dislikes stand in the way of a sane outlook on the case. I am convinced that both the young Greshams know something more than they have told. As a matter of fact, there isn't a doubt of it—they showed it clearly when they begged me to call off the investigation. We know further that they are intimate with Naomi Lawrence—and we know that either Naomi or her husband—or both—are mixed up in this case. Events dovetail too perfectly for us to ignore the fact that however right Evelyn Rogers may believe she is—she may be wrong!"

"And I'm not forgetting, either—" said Leverage grimly, "that Hazel Gresham was engaged to marry Warren!"

"No. Nor am I. It's a puzzling combination of circumstances, Leverage: a perfectly knit thing—if we don't—and so now we come to Gerald Lawrence and his wife."

Leverage did not take his cue immediately. He sat drumming a heavy tattoo on the tabletop, forehead corrugated in a frown of intensive thought. When he did speak it was in a manner well-nigh abstract–

"Gerald Lawrence probably lied when he said he didn't leave Nashville until the two a.m. train."

"He may have. One thing which impressed me about Lawrence was this, Leverage–when the man started bucking me he thought he had a perfect alibi. He was supremely confident that I was going to be completely nonplussed. It was only after I had questioned him closely that he realized his alibi was no alibi at all. He realized he couldn't prove where he was at the time the murder was committed–that for all the evidence he could adduce he might have been right here in this city."

"Yes–?"

"The significant fact is this," explained Carroll–"when he made the discovery that his alibi was no good–*he* was the most surprised person in the room!"

"And you're thinking," suggested the Chief, "that if he had actually had a hand in the murder of Warren he would have had an alibi that would have been an alibi?"

"Just about that. Get me straight, Chief–I would rather believe Lawrence guilty than any other person– except perhaps Barker–with whom I have come in contact since this investigation began. He has one of the most unpleasant personalities I have ever known. He is a congenital grouch. But he told his Nashville story so frankly–and then became so panicky with surprise when my questioning showed him that his alibi was rotten–that we must not fasten definitely upon him–"

"–Except to be pretty darn sure that he knows more about it than he has told."

"Yes. Perhaps."

"Perhaps. Ain't you sure he does?"

"I'm not sure of anything. I haven't one single item of information save that regarding the one person whom I would prefer to see left clear."

"And that is?"

"Mrs. Naomi Lawrence."

Leverage nodded agreement. "Things do look pretty tough for her."

"More so than you think, Eric." Carroll designated on his fingers, "Count the facts against her as we know them: irrespective of their weight or significance.

"First, she is a beautiful woman, twelve years younger than her husband and very unhappy in her domestic life. Second, she was very friendly with Roland Warren. Of course, Miss Rogers' fatuous belief that Warren was crazy about her is pure rot: he called at that house to see either Gerald or Naomi Lawrence. We must admit that the chances are the woman was the person in whom he was interested. Third, in substantiation of that belief we know that he frequently gave her presents. It doesn't matter how valuable the presents were—he gave them. That proves a certain amount of interest."

Carroll paused for a brief explanation. "Mind you, Leverage—I'm not trying to make out a case against Naomi Lawrence—I'm only being honest. To continue—fourth, we know that in spite of the fact that she is afraid to remain in a house alone at night, she suggested that her sister visit at the home of Hazel Gresham on the night Warren was killed. Her husband was supposed—according to his story—to be in Nashville. It is absurd to presume that when she let Evelyn go out for the night she expected to remain alone until morning. Therefore, for the sake of argument, we will assume that she knew her husband would be back that night. If that is the case—we are also forced to believe that there was something sinister about it.

"Fifth—we are fairly positive that she packed a suit-case the morning before the murder, that the suit-case left the house that morning and that two days later it mysteriously reappeared–"

"Yes," interrupted Leverage, "and we know that Warren was planning to make a trip with someone else!"

"Exactly!"

"Which makes it pretty clear," finished Leverage positively, "that Mrs. Lawrence was the woman in the taxicab!"

17
BARKER ACCUSES

The men looked at each other in silence for a minute. Leverage was sorry for Carroll—sorry because he knew that Carroll was disappointed, that the boyish detective had hoped against hope that the trail would lead to some person other than the flaming creature who was Gerald Lawrence's wife.

It was not that Carroll had become infatuated with her. It was merely that he liked her—liked her sincerely—and was sorry for her. The conclusions to be inevitably reached from the premise that Naomi was the woman in the taxicab were none too pleasant. In the first place there was the matter of morals involved. It had been pretty well established that the dead man had planned a trip to New York with someone: there was the fact that he had purchased a drawing room and two railroad tickets—only one of which later had been found in his pockets at midnight that night.

Then there was the circumstance of Mrs. Lawrence packing her suit-case and taking it, or sending it, from the house during the day—and its reappearance a couple of days later. It also explained her willingness that Evelyn spend the night with Hazel Gresham. Knowing that she, Naomi, was going to leave her home before midnight, she had not wanted her youthful sister to spend the balance of the night alone—and so had sent her to the house of a friend. That much was clear—

"It's hell!" burst out Carroll.

"You said it."

"Suppose she *was* the woman in the taxicab—?"

"Yes—suppose she was: it doesn't prove that she killed Warren?"

"No–but it proves something a good deal worse, Leverage. It proves that she was going to elope with him."

"It may–we don't *know*!"

"We don't *know* anything. But there is a certain logic which is irrefutable–and, confound it! Man–what are we going to do now?"

Leverage refused to meet his friend's eyes. "We-e-ll, David–suppose you tell me what *you* think we should do?"

"We ought to–but it's rotten! Absolutely rotten!"

"Trouble with you, David," said Leverage kindly–"is that you're too damned human!"

"I can't help it. It isn't my fault. And if I was sure that Naomi Lawrence was the woman in that taxi, I'd arrest her immediately. But I'm not sure, Leverage–and neither are you. Let's admit that it's a ten to one bet–we're still not positive. And I wonder if you realize what her arrest would mean?"

"What?"

"We can't arrest a woman of her prominence socially without a reason–and a darned good reason. Therefore, when we arrest her we have to tell the public why we're doing it. And what do we tell 'em? That she was–or might have become–Warren's light-o'-love! That she was going to elope with him!"

"And yet, David–all of that is probably true."

"Probably–yes. But not positively. We haven't proved anything. And once we explode that social bomb–we've started something that she'll never live down. We've done more than that–we've played the devil with Evelyn's chance of happiness. That kid will be in a swell position when the scandal-mongers get hold of the gossip about her sister. Can't you hear 'em–babbling about it being in the blood?"

"But she might prove that none of it is true."

"That doesn't make a bit of difference. Gossip pays no attention to a refutation. Leave consideration for Mrs. Lawrence out of it altogether–and figure where Evelyn comes in on the backwash."

"It *is* tough. But this is a murder case–and, anyway, I don't think she killed Warren."

"Even if she didn't–I fancy she'd rather be convicted of murder–than of what this will lead to. I'm afraid, Leverage. We're trifling with something a good deal more sacred than human life. If Naomi Lawrence is guilty–there's no objection to her suffering. But her kid sister will suffer too–"

"You don't think, Carroll–that she looked like that kind?"

"Good God! *No*! And even if we prove that she was the woman in the taxicab–that she was going to elope with Warren–it still won't prove that she was that kind. There's something about that husband of hers–meet him, Leverage–meet him! That's the only way you'll have any understanding of my sympathy for the wife."

Leverage rose and walked to the window. He spoke without turning, "Tough–David; mighty tough. And we've got to do something."

No answer. Carroll had lighted a cigarette and was puffing fiercely upon it. Leverage spoke again softly–

"Haven't we?"

"I suppose we have–"

"Well?"

Another long silence. "Isn't there anything we can do, Eric–before we start something that no human power can stop? Something to make us sure–to give us a clincher? That's all I ask. You say I'm cursed with too much of the milk of human kindness. Perhaps I am–perhaps that's what makes me no better detective than I am–but it's a trait–good or bad–that I'll never get over. And until every possible doubt as to that woman's complicity has been removed, I am opposed to any such course as arrest and public announcement of the reasons therefor."

Leverage shook his head. He was disappointed in his friend. Not that Carroll would flinch from duty–but Leverage considered it a weakness that Carroll insisted on postponing the inevitable. He was sorry–he knew that it had to come: Naomi's arrest and the consequent nasty publicity. His manner, as he addressed Carroll, was that of a man who washes his hands of something–

"It's your case, David. Handle it your own way. That's been our agreement always when we worked together–and I'm game to stick to it now."

Carroll flushed. "Yet you're disappointed in me?"

"A little–yes," said Leverage honestly. "But I've been disappointed in you before, David–and you've always made me sorry for it. I know you won't throw me down this time. You've never done it yet."

"You're safe!" said Carroll grimly. "No–" as Leverage started for the door; "Don't go! I want to think for a minute–"

Leverage sank obediently into a chair. Carroll paced the room slowly. He was thinking–struggling to decide upon a plan of action which would delay the arrest of Naomi Lawrence until the ultimate moment. And finally he flung back his head triumphantly. Leverage looked up with pleasure at the sound of relief in his friend's voice–

"Leverage?"

"Yes?"

"You say this case is mine–absolutely? To handle as I see fit?"

"Yes."

"You agree that we have enough against William Barker to arrest him?"

"Gosh–I said that the first day we met him."

"You also agree that he knows whatever connection the Lawrences have with the Warren murder?"

"I do."

"Then get Barker. Bring him here!"

Leverage departed with a light step. There was a smile on his lips. Here was the style of procedure with which he was familiar and in full sympathy. Here was action supplanting stagnation–something definite succeeding the long nerve-wracking period of conjecture which appeared to lead nowhere save into a labyrinth of endless discussion.

He started the machinery of the department to moving. When he returned to his office an hour later, Carroll was still seated motionlessly before the grate fire—an extinguished cigar between his teeth—eyes focused intently on the dancing flames. Leverage spoke—

"I've got Barker."

"Where is he?"

"Downstairs."

"Bring him in. You stay here when he comes—send everybody else out."

Cartwright brought Barker into the room and Leverage dismissed the plainclothesman. Barker, eyes wide with fear, face pallid—yet with a certain belligerence in his attitude—confronted the two detectives.

"I say—" he started, "what does this mean?"

"It means," said Carroll coldly, "that you are under arrest for the murder of Roland Warren!"

"That I'm—" Barker fell back a step. It was plain that he was surprised. "You're arresting *me* for Warren's murder?"

"Yes."

"But I didn't do it. I'll swear I didn't."

"Of course you'll swear it—" Carroll's steely voice excited a vast admiration in Leverage's breast. Many times before he had seen the transformation in his friend from all too human softness to almost inhuman coldness—yet he never failed of surprise at the phenomenon. "But we know you did do it."

"You don't know nothin' of the kind," Barker's voice came in a half-snarl. "I don't give a damn how smart you fly-cops are—you can't prove nothin' on me."

"That so?"

"Yes—that's so. Just because I worked for Warren ain't no reason why you should arrest me for his murder. Suppose I had wanted to kill him—and I didn't—didn't have no reason at all. But suppose I had wanted too—you know bloody well that I didn't do it."

"Why do we know that?"

"Because you know he was killed by a woman!"

"Aa-a-ah! That's what you think, eh?"

"I know a woman killed him."

"You were present?"

"Bah! Trying to trap me—are you? Well, I ain't going to be trapped. I don't know nothin' about it. Like I said from the first."

"But you do know something about it," insisted Carroll icily. "And I'd advise you to come clean with us."

"There ain't nothin' to come clean about."

"You say we know that a woman killed Warren. You seem pretty confident of that yourself. Well, we happen to know that you know who this woman was. Who was she?"

For the first time Barker's eyes shifted. "You know as well as me who she was?"

"Who was she?" Carroll's voice fairly snapped.

"It was—Miss Hazel Gresham!"

Carroll stared at the man. "Listen to me, Barker—you're lying and we know you're lying. You know as well as we do that Miss Gresham was at her own home when Warren was killed. I don't want any more lies! Not one! Now tell us the truth!"

Barker stared first at Carroll—then at Leverage. An expression of doubt crossed his face. It was patent that these men knew more than he had credited them. Finally he shrugged his shoulders—

"Well—Mr. Carroll, that bein' the case—I ain't goin' to stick my head in a noose for nobody!"

"You've decided to tell us the truth!"

"I have."

"You know who killed Roland Warren?"

"Yes—I know who killed Roland Warren!"

"Who was it?"

Barker's face went white. Leverage and Carroll leaned forward eagerly—nervously. It seemed an eternity before

Barker's answer came—but when it did, his words rang with conviction—he uttered a name—

"*Mrs. Naomi Lawrence!*"

18
"AND NOTHING BUT THE TRUTH—"

Barker's words reverberated through the room—to be succeeded by an almost unnatural stillness; a silence punctured by the ticking of the cheap clock on the mantel, by the crackling of the flames in the grate, by the whistling of the wind around the corners of the gaunt gray stone building which housed the police department.

The accused man looked eagerly upon the faces of the two detectives; then, slowly, his chest expanded with relief: he saw that they believed him.

And Carroll did believe. It was not that he wanted to—he had fought himself mentally away from that conviction time after time; had threshed over every scintilla of evidence, searching futilely for something which would clear this radiant woman whom he had met but once. Carroll's interest—however platonic—was intensely personal. The woman had impressed herself indelibly upon him. It was perhaps her air of game helplessness; perhaps the stark tragedy which he had seen reflected in her eyes when he had first entered her home and saw that she knew why he had come.

And now, driven into the corner which he had hoped to avoid, his retentive memory brought back a circumstance well-nigh forgotten. He addressed Barker, his voice soft-hopeless.

"You mean that Mrs. Lawrence was the woman in the taxicab?"

"Yes, sir." The "sir," which Barker used for the first time was respectful.

"Where had she been during the evening—after dark of the night of the—killing?"

"At home—I believe."

"You believe?"

"Yes, sir."

Carroll's eyes lighted. His voice cracked out accusingly: "Don't you *know* that that is incorrect?"

Barker shook his head. "Why, no, sir. Of course, I ain't sayin' positive that she *was* at home all evenin', but–"

"As I understand it," said Carroll slowly–"an accommodation train came in just about that time: isn't that a fact?"

"Some train came in then–I don't know which one it was."

"Isn't it a fact that the woman who got into the taxicab had been a passenger on that train: that she got off with the other passengers, carrying a suit-case?"

"There ain't nobody can see the passengers get off the trains at the Union Station, Mr. Carroll. You go down them steps and approach the waitin' room underground–crossin' under the tracks."

"But you do know that this woman–whoever she was–passed through the waiting room with the passengers who came on that train, don't you?"

"Yes, sir–she done that, but it don't mean nothin'."

"Why don't it?"

"Well, sir, for one thing–ain't it true that the papers said the suit-case she was carryin' wasn't hers at all. Ain't it a fact that she had Mr. Warren's suit-case?"

"Well?" Carroll saw his last hope glimmering.

"You see, sir–Mr. Warren was meetin' Mrs. Lawrence at the station. He got there with his suit-case at about ten minutes to twelve. She got there about ten or fifteen minutes later–"

"How did she come?"

"On the street car. And when she come out–she was alone and it was his suit-case she was carryin'–the same suit-case he had taken into the station. The one you found in the taxicab."

"I see–" Carroll did not want to believe Barker's story, but he knew that the man was telling the truth–or at least that most of what he was saying was true. The detective seemed crushed with disappointment. Leverage, seated in the corner of the room, chewing savagely on a big black cigar–was sorry for his friend: sorry–yet proud of the way he was standing the gaff of his chagrin. Carroll again spoke to Barker–manner almost apathetic–

"You know a good deal more about this thing than you've told us, don't you Barker?"

"Yes, sir."

"Very well: let's have your story from the beginning to the end. I'll be honest with you: I believe a good deal of what you've told me. Some of your story I don't believe. Other portions of it need substantiation. But you are mighty close to being charged with murder–and now is your chance to clear yourself. Go to it!"

Barker plunged a hand into his pocket. "Can I smoke, Mr. Carroll?"

"Certainly. And sit down."

They drew up their chairs before the fire. Carroll did not look at Barker, but Leverage's steady gaze was fixed on the man's crafty face.

"I'm going to come clean with you, Mr. Carroll. I'm going to tell you everythin' I know–and everythin' I think. I didn't want to do it–and I don't want to now. But I'd a heap rather have the job of convincin' you that I ain't mixed up in this murder than I would of makin' a jury believe the same thing. I reckon you'll give me a square deal."

"I will," snapped Carroll. "Go ahead."

"In the first place," started Barker slowly, "it's my personal opinion that Mr. Warren never had no idea of marryin' Miss Gresham. Maybe I'm all wrong there–but it's what I think. I can't prove that, of course–an' no one else can't either.

"Also I happen to know that he's been crazy about Mrs. Lawrence for a long time. He's been hangin' around the house a good deal–an' doin' little things like a man will when he's nuts about a woman. For instance, Mr. Warren wasn't no investing man: s'far's I know he had all his money in gover'ment bonds and such like investments. But he sank some money into them woolen mills that Mr. Lawrence owns. And also he pretended that he liked that kid sister of Mrs. Lawrence's–Evelyn Rogers. But there ain't hardly a doubt in my mind, Mr. Carroll–an' I'm handin' it to you straight–that he was crazy about Mrs. Lawrence. And, not meanin' no impertinence, sir–I ain't blamin' him a bit.

"Also, I reckon she wasn't exactly indifferent to him. She's been up in his apartment twice–which is a terrible risky thing, an' somethin' no woman will do unless she's wild about a feller. Oh! Everything was proper while she was there. I was at home all the time and I know. But she was–what you call, indiscreet–that is, in comin' up there at all–no matter how decent she acted when she was there. An' also, sir, she used to write him notes–most every day."

"You have some of those notes?"

"No, sir. I had one–if you want the truth–but when I saw you was watchin' me–sure, I know you've had a couple of dicks shadowing me–I destroyed it."

"Where are the rest of her letters?"

"Mr. Warren used to burn 'em up careful. He wasn't takin' no chances of someone findin' 'em and he bein' caught in a scandal–which is why I think he really cared about her serious. His other lady friends he used to joke about–but never Mrs. Lawrence. An' the one letter of her's that I had–I'm betting that he looked for three days without stopping before he gave it up as a bad job.

"That's the way things was when I seen him begin to make arrangements to get away from town. It wasn't supposed to be none of my business and Mr. Warren never was a feller I could ask questions of. When he had something to tell me, he told it–an' I never got nothin' out of him by askin'. But, bein' his valet, there was certain things I couldn't very well miss knowin'. I know his apartment is sublet for the new tenants to come in on the first of the month, he placed his car with a dealer to be sold and he didn't order a new one an' he drew a whole heap of cash out of the bank the day before he was killed.

"Also that day he sent me downtown to do some shoppin'. While I was downtown I seen him go into the railroad ticket office. I didn't pay much attention to that then and later on he drove by the house for a minute. I had taken his laprobe out of the car the night before and forgot to put it back—so I thought I'd better do it. I went downstairs without his knowing it—and when I put the laprobe in the car I seen he had a suit-case in there. An' the suit-case wasn't his, sir—the initials on it was N.L.—which, if you know, sir—Mrs. Lawrence's name is Naomi.

"That made things pretty clear to me then. He drove off and come back about a half hour later. I looked when he come back and the suit-case wasn't in the car no more. And it was then that he handed me a big wad of wages in advance and told me he wasn't going to need me no more and I could quit any time after five o'clock in the afternoon."

Barker paused, lighted another cigarette from the stump of the one he had been smoking—inhaled a great puff, and continued. His manner was that of a man under great mental stress—as though he was struggling to recall every infinitesimal detail which might possibly have a bearing on the case.

"That sort of carries me along to the night, sir—as I left there at five o'clock and he was still there—tellin' me goodbye and givin' me an excellent reference and sayin' I was a good valet an' all like that, sir.

"After leavin' there I went out and got some supper, and then I went up to Kelly's place and horned into an open game of pool. You know Kelly's place is pretty close to the Union Station and when it come about ten o'clock I got tired and went an' sat down in the corner, eatin' a hot dog from the stand in Kelly's–an' then I sort of got to thinkin' things over.

"An' thinkin' things over that way, Mr. Carroll–I began to think that Mrs. Lawrence was doin' a terrible foolish thing, and I was kinder sorry about it. Now don't get no idea that I'm wantin' you to believe I got a soft heart or anythin' like that–but then I sort of liked Mr. Warren and I knew Mrs. Lawrence was a decent woman– and I knew once she got on the train with Mr. Warren she was done for. And when I got to thinkin' about that, sir–it struck me that maybe somethin' could be done to keep 'em from eloping with each other that way. Not that I was plannin' to do anything–but curiosity sort of got me, and along about eleven o'clock or a little while after I went out of Kelly's and up to the Union Station. I sat down over in the corner and waited for somethin' to happen–sort of hopin' maybe I had been wrong all the time and there wasn't going to be no elopement.

"I waited there a long time, and then suddenly a taxicab came up to the curb and Mr. Warren got out. Then the taxicab beat it down-town again and Mr. Warren went in the station. And as he come in one door, I beat it out of the other."

"Why?" snapped Leverage.

"Because him seein' me there was certain to start somethin'. And I wasn't hankerin' for nothin' like that to happen. So I went across the street and tried to get shelter against the wall of that dump of a hotel over there. An' it was cold: I ain't seen such a cold night in my life. I almos' froze to death."

"And yet you continued to stand there?"

"Sure–I was curious. Kinder foolish, maybe, but I wanted to see had I figured right about him eloping with Mrs. Lawrence. So I stood there, darn near dead with the cold, when the midnight Union Station street car stopped an' Mrs. Lawrence got out. An' the first thing I noticed was that she wasn't carryin' no suit-case. I noticed that on account of havin' seen her suit-case in Mr. Warren's car that day. She didn't carry nothin' but one of these handbag things that women lug around with 'em."

"How was she dressed?"

"Fur coat and hat and a heavy veil."

"You could see the veil from across the street at midnight?"

"No sir. Not from there. But when she went in the depot, I followed across the street and looked inside to see what was goin' to happen." He paused a moment and then Carroll prodded him on—

"Well—what *did* happen?"

"The minute Mr. Warren seen her come in he beat it through the opposite door from where I was standin' out to the platform that runs parallel to the tracks. An' he nodded to her to follow him. She sort of nodded like she was wise, an' took a seat so's nobody would think anything in case there was anyone there lookin' for something. Mr. Warren walked off down the outside platform towards the baggage room an' after about three minutes she gets up, kinder casual-like and follers. Soon as she went through the door to the platform I went in the waitin' room."

"What did you do then?"

"Nothin'. Just made a bee line for the steam radiator an' tried to get warm. I was so cold it hurt. An' I stood there for about ten minutes. Then I heard that train comin' in an' I went outside into the street again."

Carroll's voice was tense. "In all that time did you hear anything—anything at all?"

Barker shook his head. "No sir—not a thing—except that train comin' in. And then the passengers from it began to come through, and I was surprised to see Mrs. Lawrence comin' with them, an' she was carryin' his suit-case."

"Whose suit-case?"

"Mr. Warren's. She come on out to the curb an' called a taxicab."

"Where was the taxicab standing?"

"Parked against the curb on Atlantic Avenue about a hundred yards from the entrance in the direction of Jackson street."

"How did she act?"

"Kinder nervous like. Noticin' her come out I seen the taxi driver when he climbed back into his cab an' when he started her up. He picked up Mrs. Lawrence an' she put the suit-case in front beside him. Then they drove off. And that's all I know sir."

Carroll rose and walked slowly the length of the room.

"What did you think when you saw Mrs. Lawrence come out of the station alone carrying Mr. Warren's suit-case? When she did that and called a taxicab and went off in it alone?"

"Not knowin' about no killin', Mr. Carroll–I thought they'd got together and talked things over an' decided to call off the elopement!"

"You did–" Carroll paused. "And the first time you knew of Warren's death?"

"Was when I read the newspapers the next morning."

"Then why," barked the detective, "did you make the blunt statement that Mrs. Lawrence killed Warren?"

"Because," said Barker simply, "I believe she did."

"How could she have killed him? When and how?"

"That's easy," explained Barker quietly. "If I'm right in thinkin' that they was goin' to call off the elopement– they could have seen that taxi standin' against the curb and he could have got in without bein' seen. It was awful dark where the taxi was standin' an' the driver says himself that he was over in the restaurant gettin' warm. So what I thought right away was that Warren got in the taxi, an' she called it. That was so they wouldn't be seen gettin' in together at that time of night. Then I thought they drove off. And then–"

"Yes–and then?"

"It was while they were alone together in that taxi, that she killed him!"

19
LABYRINTH

Long after William Barker left the room—held in custody under special guard—David Carroll and Chief of Police Eric Leverage maintained a thoughtful silence. Leverage wanted to talk—but refused to be the first to broach the subject which each knew was uppermost in the mind of the other. And it was Carroll who spoke first—

"Well, Eric," he said dully, "you called the turn that time."

"Reckon I did, David."

"It looks mighty bad for Mrs. Lawrence—mighty bad." He hesitated. "I wonder whether Barker told the truth when he said he had been calling on Mrs. Lawrence to apply for a job?"

"Why not?"

"Because when valets or butlers apply for domestic positions they don't go to the front door, and Barker did on both occasions he visited that house. No, Leverage—I don't think he told the truth there."

"Then what *was* he doing at the house?"

"Mmm! Just struck me, Eric—that he may have been trying a little private blackmail."

Leverage arched his eyebrows: "On Mrs. Lawrence?"

"Yes—on Mrs. Lawrence. You see, it's this way: according to Barker's own story he knew everything which transpired at the station. If we believe what he told us, and if he is correct in his belief that Mrs. Lawrence did the killing, then we know he is the only person who—until now—had any knowledge of the identity of the woman in the taxicab. That being the case, and Barker being obviously not a high type of man, it is certainly not unreasonable to presume that he was capitalizing his information."

"Seems plausible," grunted Leverage. "But where does it get us?"

"Just this far," explained Carroll. "Unless Barker was applying for a position at the Lawrences–where they not only do not employ a male servant, but have never employed one–he was not seeking employment anywhere. He has been taking life pretty easy, all of which is indicative of a supply of money from outside. And I fancy that Mrs. Lawrence would pay a pretty fancy price to have her name left out of this rotten scandal."

Leverage held Carroll with his eyes: "Do you believe Barker's story, David?"

"Believe it? Why, yes. Most of it anyway."

"You believe Mrs. Lawrence was the woman in the taxicab?"

"I've got to believe it."

"Do you believe she killed him?"

"Evidence points to that answer, Leverage. You see, Barker's story impressed me this way: it is the only sane, logical solution of the killing which has yet been advanced. Neither of us has ever yet hit upon an answer to the puzzle of the body in the taxicab. What Barker tells us is perfectly plausible–" Carroll paused–

"You see," he continued, "from the first I have maintained that Mrs. Lawrence is a decent woman–innately decent. I will even admit that her domestic life was so miserably unbearable that she would entertain the idea of eloping with Warren: that she went so far as to attempt to carry that idea into execution. But I am also ready–and eager, too, if you will, to believe that when she reached the stepping off place she must have reneged. That woman couldn't have done anything else.

"We are fairly well satisfied–from Barker's own story– that there had been nothing wrong in the relations between Warren and Mrs. Lawrence up to that night. But we are pretty sure that they met at the station to go away together. What is more reasonable than to presume that she lost her nerve at the eleventh hour: that, unhappy as she was at home, she was unable to take the step which would forever make her a social outcast?

"Very well. If that is true, we have them at the station at midnight. The weather is the worst of the year. They are standing in the dark passageway between the main waiting room and the baggage room. No light is on the corner of Jackson street. They see only one taxicab on duty. For all they know—the last street car has passed. They conceive the idea of making a single taxicab do double duty—and, knowing that the driver is across the street drinking coffee and getting warm—Warren gets into the cab from the blind side, Mrs. Lawrence returns to the waiting room as the accommodation rolls in, she picks up Warren's suit-case which had been left there, steps to the curb and summons the cab, in which Warren is hiding all the time. Sounds all right so far?"

"Perfectly," said Leverage. "Go ahead."

"Walters gets the signal and drives up. Mrs. Lawrence gets in. He drives away. And then—"

Leverage leaped forward eagerly: "Yes—?? And then?"

"Well," said Carroll slowly, "we don't know what happened in that taxicab. We believe that Mrs. Lawrence is a decent woman. We know that Warren would have gone through with the elopement. That being the case, we can fancy his keen disappointment. Under those circumstances, Eric—a good many things could have occurred in that taxicab which might have justified Warren's death at her hands."

Leverage crossed to his desk, from the top drawer of which he took a box of cigars. He was frowning as he recrossed to Carroll and offered him one. Then, with almost exasperating deliberation, the head of the police force clipped the end of his own cigar, held a match to it, replaced the box in his desk and took up his post before the fire—with his back to it so that he could watch Carroll's face.

"You really want to believe that story, don't you, David?" he asked gently.

"Yes."

"And yet you know it is shot all full of holes."

"How?"

"For one thing," said Leverage slowly—"how do you explain the fact that it was a.32 that killed him. Not that a .32 is any big gun—it isn't—but it does make a considerable racket."

"The shooting probably took place at the R.L.&T. crossing while the train was passing. The sound of the shot may have been drowned in the roar of the train—not entirely smothered of course, but sufficiently blended with the other noise not to attract the attention of the half-frozen driver. And, the cab being stopped there, it must have been at that point that Mrs. Lawrence—panicky over what had occurred—left the taxi."

"You're a dandy little ol' explainer, Carroll. But you've forgotten one other important item."

"What is it?"

"The address Mrs. Lawrence gave—981 East End Avenue. That address was a stall—we know it was a stall. We were hot on that end of it the night the body was found. And if those two people were trying to get home, Carroll—if Warren was already in the cab and Mrs. Lawrence gave the address—and if she wanted to get away from Warren and safe at home as soon as she could—she'd never have ordered Walters to drive to 981 East End avenue!"

Carroll did not answer. There was no answer possible. Leverage's logic was irrefutable. And finally Carroll rose to his feet and slipped into his heavy overcoat. Leverage's eyes were turned kindly upon him.

"Where are you going, David!"

"I'm going to play my last trump. If it doesn't uncover something—I throw up my hands. Laugh at me if you will,

Eric–rail at me for being chicken-hearted, for playing hunches too strongly–but I have an idea that Mrs. Lawrence did not kill Warren. Don't ask me how or why? I don't know–I admit that frankly. But I've always banked on my knowledge of human nature, Leverage–and my instinct has never yet betrayed me. Just now it is forcing me to give this woman every chance in the world to clear herself. I am hoping that circumstances will allow me to bring this case to a conclusion without making public her connection with it–the elopement she was planning."

"You do believe that part of the story, then: that she was going to elope with Warren?"

"I do. I don't want to–but I'm honest with myself."

"Then," exclaimed Leverage with a slight touch of exasperation in his manner–"who in thunder could have killed Warren if she didn't? And when?"

"That," said Carroll simply, "is what I hope to find out."

"From where?"

"From the lips of Mrs. Lawrence. I'm going to have a talk with her."

Carroll was far from happy during his drive to the Lawrence home. The Warren mystery seemed to be verging on a solution, but in Carroll's breast there was none of the pardonable surge of elation which normally was his under these circumstances. It had been a peculiar case from the first. The *dramatis personae* had all been of the better type, with the single exception of William Barker–they had been persons against whom the detective was loath to believe ill. And, most eagerly, he had shied from the belief that Mrs. Lawrence was connected in a sinister way with the death of Roland Warren.

Yet he found himself en-route to her home, facing the ordeal of an interview with her–an ordeal for her as well as for him–and one through which he feared she could not safely come. For, frankly as Carroll had admitted to his friend that he hoped to find Naomi innocent–he was yet honest and fearless, and failure of the woman to clear herself meant her arrest. Carroll was determined upon that–yet he dreaded it as a child dreads the dentist–as something painful beyond belief.

He rang the bell–then groaned as Evelyn Rogers greeted him effusively. She ushered him ostentatiously into the parlor and drew up a chair close to his–

"Mr. Carroll–it's just simply *scrumptuous* of you to call on me informally like this. I can't tell you how tickled I am. I was sitting upstairs, simply bored to extinction. Sis has been a terrible drag on me recently–really you'd have thought there had been a death in the family. Or something! It's been simply graveyardy! And now you come in–like a darling angel–and save me from the willywoggles. You're a *dear*, and–"

"But–but–I really came to see your sister."

"Oh! *pff*! That's what poor dear Roland used to say all the time. But I always knew I was the one he wanted to see. Goodness, he was simply *crazy* about me–but of course Sis never understood that. She hasn't yet realized that I'm grown up."

"Peculiar how blind some folks are. But this time, Miss Rogers–I really do want to chat with your sister. Not that I wouldn't prefer a talk with you. So if you'll tell her I'm here–and would like to see her *privately*–"

Evelyn rose and started reluctantly toward the door. "I suppose it's up to me to make myself very scarce. But it is simply *precious* of you to admit you'd rather talk to me. Poor Roland used to say that–but he always said it as though he was kidding. I believe *you*!"

"I assure you I'm serious."

"I know it. And anyway, I was thinking of running out for a minute–and I suppose this is a good chance. Of course, I'd stay and see you if you wanted–but I suppose you've got something terribly dry to discuss and so–"

She left the room and Carroll heaved a sigh of infinite relief. A few minutes later the hall door swung back and Naomi and Evelyn entered. He was immensely relieved to see that the youngster was cloaked for the street and murmured a few idle words to her before she went. And until the front door banged behind her he remained standing before the fireplace, his eyes focused on the tragic figure of Naomi.

She faced him bravely enough, but in her eyes he read the message of knowledge. There was no need for words between them. She knew why he had come–and he knew that she knew.

"Sit down, please, Mr. Carroll."

He waited until she had seated herself and then followed suit. He controlled his voice with an effort–his words came softly, reassuringly.

"I'm sorry I've come this way, Mrs. Lawrence. I've come–"

"I know why you have come, Mr. Carroll. You need not mince matters."

He drew a long breath. "Isn't it true, Mrs. Lawrence, that *you* were the woman in the taxi-cab the night Mr. Warren was killed?"

She inclined her head. "Yes."

Carroll fidgeted nervously. "I must warn you to be careful in what you say to me, my friend. I am the detective in charge of this case, and–"

"There is no use in concealment, Mr. Carroll. I have been driven almost crazy since that night. I have almost reached the end of my rope. It was the scandal I have been fighting to avoid–not so much for my own sake as for Evelyn and my husband. Publicity–of this kind–would be very–very–awkward–for both of them."

"I'm sorry–" Carroll hesitated. "If you don't care to talk to me–"

She shrugged slightly. "It makes no difference–now. I'd rather talk to you than someone who might understand less readily–or more harshly."

"I may question you?"

"Yes."

"I regret it–and rest assured that I am trying to find– a way out–for you."

"There is no way out–from the scandal. But that is my own fault–"

Somewhere down the block an auto horn shrieked: in another room of the house an old grandfather's clock chimed sonorously.

"You admit that you were the woman in the taxicab?"

"Yes. Certainly."

"Do you admit that you killed Roland Warren?"

Her startled eyes flashed to his. The color drained from her cheeks. Her answer was almost inaudible–

"No!"

"You did not kill him?" Carroll was impressed with the nuance of truth in her answer.

"No–I did not kill him."

"But when you got into the taxicab–isn't it a fact that he was already there?"

"Yes–he was there, Mr. Carroll. *But he was already dead!*"

20
A CONFESSION

"–Already dead!" Carroll did not know if his lips framed the words or if the walls of the room had echoed. He was startled at a time when he fancied that there could be no further surprise in store for him. He found himself eyeing the woman and he wondered that he gave credence to her statement.

Naomi was sitting straight, large black eyes dilated, hands gripping the arms of the chair tightly, lips slightly parted. Even under the stress of the moment Carroll was actually conscious of her feminine allure; unable to free himself of her hypnotic personality. She spoke–but he scarcely heard her words through his chaos of thought.

"He was dead–before I got into the taxi-cab."

He saw that she was fighting to impress upon him the truth of her well-nigh unbelievable statement, that every atom of her brain strove desperately to convince him. And then she relaxed suddenly, as though from too great strain, and a shudder passed over her.

"I knew–I knew–"

"You knew *what*, Mrs. Lawrence?"

"I knew that you would not believe me. Oh! It's true– this story I am telling you. But I knew no one could believe it–it stretches one's credulity too far. That is why I have kept silent through all these days which have passed–that and a desire to save Evelyn and my husband."

"You love your husband?" Carroll bit his lips. The question had slipped out before he realized that he had formed the words. But she did not evade the issue–

"I despise him, Mr. Carroll. But he has played square with me—more so than I have with him. And publication of this would hurt him—"

"Because he cares for you?"

"No. But because he is proud: because he is jealous of his personal possessions—of which I am one."

"I see—And Mr. Warren—?"

She spread her hands in a helpless, hopeless gesture. "What's the use, Mr. Carroll? Why, should I wrack myself with the story when you do not even believe the reason upon which it is based? If you only believed me when I tell you that when I got into the taxicab Roland had already been killed—"

"I do believe that," returned Carroll gently.

She inbreathed sharply, then her eyes narrowed a trifle. "Do you mean that—or is it bait to make me talk?"

"I can not do more than repeat my statement. I believe what you have told me."

She held his eyes for a moment, then slowly hers shrank from the contact. "You are telling me the truth," she ventured.

"And if you will tell me the whole story, Mrs. Lawrence—I shall see what I can do for you."

"What is there to do for me? There is no way to keep my name from it—my name and the story of the mistake which I made—was willing to make."

"Good God! No."

"If we—" he used the pronoun unconsciously—"can establish that, there may be some way of keeping the details from the public. Suppose you start at the beginning—and tell me what there is to tell?"

She hesitated. "Everything?"

"Everything—or nothing. A portion of the story will not help either of us. Of course you don't have to—"

Impulsively she leaned forward. "There is something about you, Mr. Carroll, which makes me trust you. I feel that you are a friend rather than an enemy."

He bowed gratefully. "Thank you."

"It really began shortly after my marriage to Mr. Lawrence—" she had started her story before she knew it. "I knew that I had made a mistake. He is nearly thirteen years older than I—a man of icy disposition, a nature which is cruel in its frigidity. I am not that—that kind of a woman, Mr. Carroll. I should not have married that type of man.

"He was good enough to me in his own peculiar way. I have a little money of my own: he is wealthy. He liked to dress me up and show me off. He was liberal with money—if not with kindness—when there was trouble in my family. After my parents died he allowed Evelyn to live with us. They have never liked one another—the more reason why I am grateful to him for allowing her to remain in the house.

"That is the life we have led together. We have long since ceased to have anything in common. He has kept to himself and I have remained alone. So far as the world knew—our home life was tranquil. Unbearably so—to a nature like mine which loves love—and life.

"I grew to hate my husband as a man much as I admired him in certain ways for his brain and his achievement. Our individualities are millions of miles apart. There was no oneness in our married life. And gradually he learned that I hated him—and he became contemptuous. That stung my pride. He didn't care. I felt—felt unsexed!

"No need to go into further detail. Sufficient to say that I became desperate for a little affection, a little kindness, a little recognition of the fact that I am a woman—and a not entirely unattractive one. It was about then that I met Roland Warren.

"I wonder if you understand women, Mr. Carroll? I wonder if it is possible for you to comprehend their psychological reactions? Because if you cannot—you will never understand what Roland Warren meant to me. You will never understand the condition which has led to–this tragedy."

She paused and Carroll nodded. "You can trust me to understand."

"I believe you do. I believe you understand something of what was going on within me when Roland came into my life. In the light of what has transpired, the fact that I was neglected by my husband seems absurd–trivial. But it is not absurd–it is *not* trivial!

"Mr. Warren was kind to me. He was attentive–courteous–I believe that he really loved me. I may have been fooled, of course. Starved as I was for the affection of a man, I may have been blind to the sincerity of his protestations. But I believed him.

"As to how I felt toward him: I don't know. I liked him–admired him. I believe that I loved him. But again we are faced with the abnormal condition in which I found myself. I believe I loved him as I believe he loved me. He represented a chance for life when for three years I had been dead–living and breathing–yet dead as a woman. And that is the most terrible of all deaths.

"We planned to elope. Don't ask me how I could consider such a thing. There is no answer possible. It wasn't a sane decision–but I decided that I would. There was the craving to get away from things–to try to start over. To revel in the richest things of life for awhile. I was selfish–unutterably so. I didn't think then of the effect on my husband–or of the effect on Evelyn. I was selfish–yes. But immoral–no! What I planned to do–under the circumstances–was not immoral. Even yet I cannot convince myself that it was.

"Roland laid all his plans to leave the city. In all my delirium of preparation–the hiding and the secrecy–I felt sincerely sorry for only one person, and that person was Hazel Gresham to whom Mr. Warren was engaged. I believe she was in love with him. But so was I–and if he loved me–as I said before, Mr. Carroll–I was selfish!

"On the morning of the day we were to go—my husband was in Nashville, you know—Mr. Warren came to the house in his car. He showed me that he had reserved a drawing-room for us to New York. In order that we would not be seen together, he gave me one of the railroad tickets. I was to reach the Union Station ten minutes before train time. If you recall—the train on which we were to go was quite late that night.

"We planned not to talk to one another at the station until after boarding the train. Morning would have published news of the scandal broadcast, but until the irrevocable step had been taken—we determined to avoid gossip. And, Mr. Carroll—I was then—what is called a 'good woman'. My faithlessness up to that time, and to this moment, had been mental—and mental only.

"When he left me that morning he took with him my suit-case. We had agreed that I was not to take a trunk: that I was to buy—a trousseau—in New York. I looked upon it almost as a honeymoon. He took my suit-case to the Union Station and checked it there. I did not see him again that day."

"Toward evening—knowing that my husband was not due back until the following morning, and realizing that I could not leave Evelyn alone in the house—I suggested that she spend the night with Hazel Gresham. She was surprised—knowing that I dread to be alone at night—but was ready enough to go. I was not overcome with either emotion or shame when I told her good-bye that afternoon. I was so hungry for happiness that I was dead to the other emotions.

"I went to the station that night in a street car. I had telephoned in advance and learned that the train was late. The night was the worst of the winter—bitterly cold. When I reached the station, I saw that Roland was already there, and as he saw me enter, he left through the opposite door—walking out to the platform which parallels the railroad tracks.

"Then from the outside, he motioned me to follow. He wanted to talk to me, but would not risk doing so where we might be seen. I sat down for awhile, then, as casually as I could, followed him onto the station platform. I saw him down at the far end near the baggage room. Again he motioned to me to follow him. And he started out past the baggage room into the railroad yards.

"I was very grateful to him. He was taking no risk of our being seen together. I followed slowly–not seeing him, but knowing that he would be waiting for me out there. You understand where I mean? It is in that section of the railroad yards where through trains leave their early morning Pullmans–the tracks are parallel to Atlantic Avenue–and also the main line tracks running into the Union Station shed.

"I was conscious of the intense cold, but excitement buoyed me up. I passed through the gate which ordinarily bars passengers from the tracks, but which that night had either been left open or opened by Roland. The wind, as I stepped from under the shelter of the station shed, was terrific: howling across the yards, stinging with sleet. It was very slippery under foot–I had to watch closely. And I was just a trifle nervous because here and there through the yards I could see lanterns–yard workers and track walkers, I presume. And occasionally the headlight of a switch engine zigzagged across the tracks–I was afraid I'd be caught in the glare–

"Finally, I saw Warren. He had walked about a hundred and fifty yards down the track and was standing in the shelter of the Pullman office building. It was very dark there–just enough light for me to make out his silhouette. I started forward–then stopped: frightened.

"For I distinctly saw the figure of a man coming into the yards from Atlantic Avenue. From the moment I noticed him I had the peculiar impression that the man had not only seen Mr. Warren and intended speaking to him–but also that the meeting was not unexpected. I stopped where I was and strained my eyes through the darkness–

"I could not see much–save that they were talking. Of course I could hear nothing. I was shivering–but more with premonition of tragedy than with the terrific cold. Then suddenly I saw the two shadows merge–the combined shadow whirled strangely. I knew that Mr. Warren was fighting with this other man.

"I started forward again. Then I saw one of the shadows step back from the other. There was the flash of a revolver–no noise, because a train was rolling under the shed at the moment. But I saw the flash of the gun. I stood motionless, horrified. I didn't advance, didn't run–

"I knew that the man who had been shot was Mr. Warren. I didn't know what to do. I felt suddenly lost; hopeless–And watching, I saw one figure stoop and lift the prostrate man. He dragged him across the tracks to the inky darkness between the Pullman offices and the rear of the baggage room. I don't know what he did there– but I remember looking toward Atlantic Avenue and seeing a yellow taxicab parked against the curb. I could see that there was no one in the driver's seat–and while I watched I saw the man who had done the shooting drag Mr. Warren's body to the taxicab. It was dark in the street–the arc light on the corner was out–

"I saw him throw Mr. Warren's body into the taxicab. It was then that I turned and fled toward the station.

"I can't tell you how I felt. At a time like that one doesn't pause to analyze one's emotional reactions. I was conscious of horror–of that and the idea that I must save myself. And then the thought struck me that perhaps Mr. Warren was *not* dead. Perhaps he was only badly wounded. If that were the case I knew that he would freeze to death in the cab. It was necessary to get to him–

"By that time I had reached the waiting room. I saw his suit-case–and then, Mr. Carroll–I thought of something else: something which made it imperative that I get to Mr. Warren–" She stopped suddenly.

Carroll–eyes wide with interest–motioned her on.

"You thought of something–something which made it necessary for you to get to him?"

"Yes. I remembered that he had in his pocket the check for my suit-case! He had checked it himself that day. I realized in a flash that there would be a police investigation–and the minute that checkroom stub was found, the detectives would have followed it up. They would have discovered my suit-case. My name would then have been indelibly linked with his–in–in that way–

"So there were two reasons why I knew I must get into that taxicab: to recover the suit-case check–and to either assure myself that he was dead, or else take him where he could get expert medical attention. Almost before I knew what I was doing I seized his suit-case, which he had left on the floor of the waiting room. I left the station along with several passengers who had come in on the local train. I called the taxicab–I told him to drive me to some place on East End Avenue–gave him some address which I knew was a long distance away–so that I would have time to learn if he was dead–and if he wasn't, to get him to a doctor's; and if he was, to find the check–the finding of which in his pocket would have connected me with the affair.

"He was dead!" She paused–choked–and went on gamely. "I got out of the taxicab when it slowed down at a railroad crossing. I walked half the distance back to town, then caught the last street car home–"

Her voice died away. Carroll relaxed slowly. Then a puzzled frown creased his forehead–

"The man who did the actual shooting," he said quietly–"have you the slightest idea as to his identity?"

"No." Her manner was almost indifferent: the strain was over–she was hardly conscious of what she was saying. "He was smaller than Mr. Warren–a man of about my husband's size–"

She stopped abruptly! Carroll's gaze grew steely—he made a note of the expression of horror in her eyes.

"About your husband's size!" he repeated softly.

21
CARROLL DECIDES

For a moment she was silent. It was patent that she was groping desperately for the correct thing to say. And finally she extended a pleading hand–

"Please–don't think that!"

"What?"

"That is was–was my husband. He wouldn't–"

"Why not?"

"Anyway–it is impossible. He was in Nashville. He didn't get home until morning."

Carroll shook his head. "I hope he can prove he was in Nashville. We have tried to prove it, and we cannot. And you must admit, Mrs. Lawrence, that had he known what you planned he would have had the justification of the unwritten law–"

Her eyes brightened. "You think, then–that if he did– he would be acquitted?"

"Yes. More so in view of your story that there was a fight between the two men. That would probably add self-defense to his plea. However, I may be wrong in that–"

"You are indeed, Mr. Carroll. My husband–isn't that kind of a man. And even if he had done the shooting–he could not have concealed it from me for this length of time. He would have given a hint–"

"No-o. He wouldn't have done that. If he shot Warren he would have been afraid of telling even you."

She walked to the window where she stood for a moment looking out on the drear December day. Then she turned tragically back to Carroll.

"You are going to arrest me?"

"No."

"Why not?"

"Because I believe your story, Mrs. Lawrence. And so long as there is any way to keep your name clear of the whole miserable mess, I shall do so."

"But if you arrest my husband—"

"I have no intention of doing that, either—unless I am convinced that he was in the city when the shooting occurred. I am not in favor of indiscriminate arrests. In this case, they can do nothing but harm."

"You are very good," she said softly. "I didn't imagine that a detective—"

"Some of us are human beings, Mrs. Lawrence. Is that so strange?"

She did not answer, and for several minutes they sat in silence—each intent in thought. It was Carroll who broke the stillness:

"Do you know William Barker?"

"Barker? Why, yes—certainly. He was Mr. Warren's valet."

"I know it. Have you seen Barker since the night Mr. Warren was killed?"

"Yes." He could scarcely distinguish her answer. "Twice."

"He called here?"

"Yes."

"Was your husband at home on either occasion?"

"No."

"Why did he come here?"

She hesitated, but only for the fraction of a second. "It was Barker who was driving me to distraction. He knew that I was the woman in the taxicab. He really believes that I killed Mr. Warren. He has been blackmailing me."

"A-ah! So *that* explains his visits, and his plentiful supply of money?"

"Yes. Oh! It was shameful—that I should be so helpless before his demands. It didn't matter that I had nothing to do with the killing—it was enough that I had to pay any price to keep my name clear of scandal. Looking back on the affair now, Mr. Carroll—I cannot understand my own weakness. But I felt that I owed it to my husband and my sister to protect them from scandal at any cost—and I have paid Barker a good deal of money—"

"I see." Carroll rose. "I want you to understand, Mrs. Lawrence, that you have helped me tremendously. And to know, also, that I shall probably succeed in keeping your name out of any disclosures which might have to be made to the public."

"But if my husband did it—"

"In that event, it will be impossible not to tell."

"And if he didn't do it?"

"Then you will be safe. But," finished the detective seriously, "if your husband didn't do it—I don't know who did. I have followed every possible trail and unless guilt can be fastened on either your husband or Barker, there isn't the faintest shadow of suspicion attached to anyone else. It will make things very difficult—for me."

During his ride to headquarters Carroll was busy with his thoughts. He was worried about the possible complicity of Gerald Lawrence in the shooting of Warren. He was more than halfway convinced that Lawrence knew a good deal about it—and the obvious method was to order Lawrence's arrest and make him prove an alibi. But such a procedure was impossible in view of his determination to protect Naomi's name to the ultimate moment.

He was greeted at headquarters by a reporter for one of the two evening papers. The reporter was eager for an interview. There had been an appalling dearth of local news, and the Warren story had been long since played beyond the point of public interest. The readers, explained the reporter, were growing tired of theories and column after column of conjecture. They wanted a few facts.

Carroll shook his head. "Nothing definite to give out yet."

The reporter was persistent. "You have made no new discoveries at all?"

"Well—I'd hardly say that."

"Then you *have*?"

"Yes," answered Carroll frankly, "I have."

"You think you know who killed Warren?"

Carroll, his mind still busy with Naomi's story, answered casually. "I believe I do. That is just a belief, mind you. But there is an outside chance that there will be important developments within the next twenty-four hours."

"Something definite, eh?"

"If anything at all happens, it will be definite."

Then Carroll excused himself and sought Eric Leverage. Under pledge of secrecy he told Leverage the entire story as he had heard it from Naomi Lawrence's lips. When he finished Leverage slammed his hand on the arm of his chair—

"Gerald Lawrence, or I'm a bum guesser," he stated positively.

"Looks that way," admitted Carroll. "What I hate about the idea is that if Lawrence is the man there will be no way on earth to keep Mrs. Lawrence's name out of it."

"You're right—How about Barker?"

"I believe Barker's story. So does Mrs. Lawrence. She believes that Barker thinks she killed Warren in the taxi."

Leverage glanced keenly at his friend. "You are going to arrest Lawrence?"

"No-o. Not yet. He may not have done it—"

"Well," sizzled the chief of police, "if he didn't and Barker didn't—who the devil did?"

Carroll shook his head hopelessly. "I don't know, Eric. If neither of those two men did, we'll be left hopelessly in the air."

"Exactly. We know that one of 'em did the shooting. We've covered this case from every angle, and if we believe that the shooting was not done by Mrs. Lawrence, we must suspect one of the two men involved. And if you are sure it wasn't Barker—"

"Let's wait a little while longer," counseled Carroll. "I want to be absolutely sure of my ground."

The two men sat in Leverage's office and talked. They discussed the case again from the beginning to its present status—threshing out each detail in the hope that they might have overlooked some vital fact which would give them a basis upon which to proceed. Their efforts were fruitless. The investigation had developed results—true enough—but those results were not at all satisfactory.

And it was about an hour later that a knock came on the door. In response to Leverage's summons, an orderly entered. In his hand he carried an evening paper—

"Just brought this in, sir. Thought you and Mr. Carroll might like to read it."

The orderly retired. Carroll spread the paper—then did something very rare. He swore profoundly. His eyes focused angrily on the enormous first page headlines:

"CARROLL HAS SOLVED WARREN MYSTERY

"Identity of Clubman's Slayer Known to Famous Detective

"WILL MAKE ARREST WITHIN 24 HOURS

"Sensational Developments Promised by David Carroll in Exclusive Interview with Reporter for The Star."

It all came back to Carroll now. The eager reporter, the news-hunger, his non-committal statements. He read furiously through the story. It proved to be one of those newspaper masterpieces which uses an enormous number of words and says nothing. Carroll was quoted as saying only what he had actually said. It was the personal conjecture of the reporter writing the story which had given spur to the vivid imagination of the headline writer.

"So now," questioned Leverage–"what are you going to do: deny it?"

"No!" snapped Carroll–"I can't. He hasn't misquoted a single line of what I said. It just makes things–makes 'em mighty embarrassing."

He sat hunched in his chair staring at the screaming headlines and re-reading the lurid story. Again an orderly entered.

"Young lady out there," he announced, "who wants to know if Mr. Carroll is here."

Instantly the mind of the detective leaped to the tragic figure of Naomi Lawrence. "She wants to see me?" he questioned.

"Yes, sir."

"Show her in." He motioned to Leverage to remain. The orderly disappeared–and in a minute, the door opened and a woman entered. Carroll sprang to his feet with an exclamation of surprise.

"Miss Gresham!"

Hazel Gresham nodded. She advanced toward Carroll. Every drop of color had been drained from her cheeks. Her manner indicated intense nervous strain. Her eyes were wide and fixed–

"I would like to speak to you alone, Mr. Carroll."

"Yes–This is Chief Leverage, Miss Gresham."

Leverage acknowledged the introduction and would have left but the girl stopped him. "On second thought, Mr. Leverage–you might remain."

Eric paused. His eyes sought Carroll's face. Both men knew that something vitally unexpected was about to be disclosed. They waited for the girl to speak–and when she did her voice was so low as to be almost unintelligible.

"About a half hour ago, gentlemen–I read the story in The Star. I–I–" she faltered for a moment, then went bravely on–"I came right down–to save you the trouble of sending for me!"

Silence: tense–expectant. "You did *what*?" queried Carroll.

"I came down—to save you the trouble—the embarrassment—of sending for me." She looked at them eagerly. "I have come to give myself up!"

Carroll frowned. "For what?"

"For—for the murder of—Roland Warren!"

The detective shook his head. "I don't understand, Miss Gresham. Really I don't. Do you mean to tell me that *you* were the woman in the taxicab?"

She was biting her lips nervously. "Yes."

"And that you shot Roland Warren?"

"Y-yes—And when I read in the paper that you knew who did it—I came right down here. I didn't want to—to—to be brought down—in a patrol wagon."

"I see—" Wild thoughts were chasing one another through Carroll's brain. He was beginning to see light. "You are quite *sure* that you killed Mr. Warren?"

"Yes, I'm sure. Why do you doubt me? Don't you suppose that I know whether I killed him? Don't you suppose I can prove that I did it—"

"Yes—I suppose you can. I wonder, Miss Gresham," and Carroll's voice was very, very gentle, "if you would wait in that room yonder for a few minutes?"

"Certainly—" She raised her head pleadingly: "You *do* believe me, don't you?"

Carroll dodged the issue. "I want to think."

Alone with Leverage, Carroll clenched his fist—"If that isn't the most peculiar—"

"She's not telling the truth, is she, David?"

"Certainly not. She couldn't smash her own alibi if she tried a million years."

He paced the room, walking in quick, jerky steps. Finally his face cleared and he stopped before Leverage's chair.

"I've got it!" he announced triumphantly.

"Got what?"

"Never mind," Carroll was surcharged with suppressed excitement. "I want you to do something for me, Leverage—and do it promptly."

"Sure—"

"Send Cartwright and bring Garry Gresham here."

"Garry Gresham?"

"Yes—the young lady's brother."

Leverage was bewildered. "What in the world do you want with him?"

"I want him," explained Carroll confidently—"because *Garry Gresham is the man who shot Warren!*"

22
THE PROBLEM IS SOLVED

Within an hour Garry Gresham appeared at headquarters in the company of Cartwright. The officer left the room and the three men were alone.

Gresham's manner was nervous, but he showed no fright. Leverage, regarding him keenly, found reason to doubt Carroll's positive statement that Gresham was the person they sought. The young man stood facing them bravely, waiting–

"Gresham," said Carroll softly, "Your sister is in that room yonder. She read the afternoon paper–the report that I knew who killed Roland Warren. She immediately came here to give herself up."

An expression of utter bewilderment crossed young Gresham's face. Then he started forward angrily: "Why are you lying to me–"

"Easy, Gresham–easy there. I am not lying to you."

He saw Garry's eyes dart to the door behind which the sister was seated. "What did she give herself up for, Carroll?"

"For killing Roland Warren."

Gresham took a firm grip on himself. "She didn't do it," he stated positively.

"Of course not," returned Carroll with equal assurance. "*You* did! And so that you will be quite convinced that I am not trying to trick you into the confession which I am sure you will make–" He crossed the room and flung open the door. "Come in, please, Miss Gresham."

The girl entered quietly–then saw her brother. Instantly her manner softened. She stepped swiftly to his side and took his hand in hers.

"Please, Garry—"

Gresham smiled; a tender, affectionate smile.

"Good scout, aren't you, Sis? But tell me," his tone was conversational, "how did you know that I shot Roland Warren?"

"You didn't!" She flung around on Carroll—"Don't believe him. I shot Mr. Warren—"

"I knew from the first that you didn't do it, Miss Gresham. I know that Miss Rogers spent the night with you. More than that, I know the identity of the woman in the taxicab."

"Who was she?" It was Gresham who questioned.

Carroll shook his head. "It doesn't matter who she was, Gresham. We're going to keep her name out of this case. She was a woman who loved Roland Warren—and his death saved her from a great mistake. There's no necessity to ruin her life, is there?"

"How did you know—it was Garry—who did the shooting?" asked the girl.

"The minute you confessed," answered the detective quietly, "I knew that you were doing it to shield someone. You could have had no possible motive for shielding either of the other two men under suspicion. I knew that it must be your brother. He had motive enough—he knew that you were in love with Mr. Warren—engaged to him. He knew that Warren was about to elope with another woman, that it would cause you intense misery. So he went to the station that night to prevent the elopement. Isn't that so, Gresham?"

The young man nodded. "Yes. When I went to your apartment the morning after the killing, it was for the purpose of confessing. But then when you assured me that my sister was not under suspicion—I decided to wait awhile before saying anything." He paused—"And as to that night—I parked my car a couple of blocks away and walked to the station through Jackson Street, intending to cut through the yards and approach the waiting room from the passenger platform. I had no idea that—that there would be—a tragedy. I wanted to reason with Warren; to beg him to save my sister from suffering which I knew would be attendant on—his elopement.

"He was walking in the yards as I entered from between the Pullman building and the baggage room. I don't know what he was doing there—but I spoke to him. He seemed startled at seeing me. I told him that I knew he was planning to elope—and begged him to call it off.

"Much to my surprise, he immediately got nasty. He seemed to want to get rid of me. He told me it was none of my damned business what he was doing. He even admitted the truth of what I said.

"That was the first hint of unpleasantness. But it grew—rapidly. He cursed me—anyway we had a brief, violent quarrel. He said something about my sister and I struck him. He clinched with me. We were fighting then— and I am a fairly good athlete. I broke out of a clinch and hit him pretty hard. He reached into his pocket and pulled a revolver. I managed to grab his hand before he could fire. I got it from him, and as I jerked it away—it went off. He fell—

"I was afraid then—panicky. I felt his body and realized that he was dead. A train had just come into the yards and there were switch engines puffing here and there—I was apprehensive that one of their headlights would pick me up. And there were some railroad men walking around the yards with lanterns in their hands. There was danger that I was going to be seen—and, had I been, I felt that I wouldn't have a leg to stand on; alone in such a place with the body of a man whom I admitted having shot—

"You see, I couldn't even prove the contemplated elopement. Late that evening I had received an anonymous telephone call from a man telling me that if I wanted to save my sister a good deal of unpleasant gossip, I'd better meet that midnight train as Warren was eloping on it with some other woman. But the man who gave me this information cut off before telling me the name of the woman. I didn't know it then—and I don't know it now.

"I knew I had to hide Warren's body; not that my killing was not justified on the grounds of self-defense, but because I would not bring my sister's name into it— and also because even if I did, there'd be no proof of the truth of what I said.

"I dragged his body into the shadows between the two buildings. Atlantic Avenue was deserted. At the curb I saw a yellow taxicab and noticed that the driver was in the restaurant across the street. I conceived the idea of putting the body in the taxicab—I knew I wouldn't be seen doing it, and it would serve the purpose of causing the body to be discovered at some point other than that at which the shooting occurred.

"I did it. Then I left. The next morning I read of the case in the papers and I have followed it closely since. I knew you were ostensibly on the wrong track and as a matter of self-preservation I determined to keep my mouth shut unless it happened that the wrong person was accused. Had you charged someone else with the killing I assure you I would have come forward. But meanwhile—not even knowing the identity of the woman in the taxi—there seemed no necessity for running the risk. There was nothing save my own word to prove self-defense, you see."

"There is now," said Carroll. Hazel started eagerly and he smiled upon her. "The story of the woman who actually was in the taxicab substantiates yours, Gresham. She had followed Warren into the yards to talk to him. She saw the whole affair from a distance—and then went back through the waiting room of the station and called the taxi in which you had placed Warren's body."

"Then Garry will be freed?" cried the girl hopefully: "His plea of self-defense will acquit him?"

"Undoubtedly," retorted Carroll. "Don't you think so, Leverage?"

"Surest thing you know," returned the chief heartily. "And I'm darned glad of it!"

Garry faced his sister. "How did you know that I had killed him, Sis?"

"I didn't," she answered quietly. "Not at first, anyway. But, if you remember, you came in the house a little after eleven o'clock that night and seemed excited. You came to my room—"

"I was thinking then," explained Garry, "that maybe *you* were eloping with Warren."

"Then you came home again a little after one o'clock. You waked me then—and acted peculiarly."

"I was reassuring myself," he said, "that you really hadn't left the house."

"The next morning while you were taking your shower I was putting up your laundry," Hazel went on. "I found a revolver in your drawer. I didn't think anything of it then—I hadn't even read the papers about the—the—killing. But later, I remembered it. I went back to look for the revolver—just why, I don't know—and it was gone. I questioned you about it a couple of days later, and you denied that you had ever had a revolver in the house. And I knew then, Garry—I knew that you had done it."

He squeezed her hand. "We always did know more about each other than we were told, didn't we, Little Sis? Because at that moment, too, I knew that you knew!"

The young man turned back to the detectives—"And what now?" he questioned.

"We'll have to hold you, Gresham. You'll have to go through the form of a trial—but you'll get off, don't worry!"

Sister and brother left the room hand-in-hand. Alone again, the two detectives faced each other. "You win, David," said Leverage admiringly. "Though darned if I know how you do it?"

"A combination of luck and common sense," returned Carroll simply. "This time it was principally luck. It usually is in such cases—but most detectives don't admit it. It is the wild-eyed reporter with the vivid imagination whom we can thank for this solution. It was his fiction that brought about Miss Gresham's ridiculous confession and that which caused me to know that she must be shielding her brother. As to how matters stand—I say Thank God!"

"Why?"

"Garry Gresham will undoubtedly be freed; it was a clear case of self-defense. Unfortunately, the fact that there was an elopement will have to be known—but that is a comparatively trivial thing, unpleasant as it may be for Miss Gresham. And, most of all—I'm glad because Naomi Lawrence's name will not be dragged into it."

"How will you work that, David?"

"It can be done, Eric. The district attorney is a pretty good friend of mine—and he's a good square fellow. Of course he will have to know the entire story; and it is a certainty that he will believe it. And when he does—you know that he will handle the case so that Mrs. Lawrence will not be connected. Irregular—yes. But you believe he can—and will—do it, don't you?"

"You bet your bottom dollar he will. He's another nut like you—so bloomin' human it hurts."

"And now—" said Carroll, "I want to chat with William Barker. There are one or two loose ends I want to clear up."

Barker was very humble as he entered the room.

"You're free of the murder charge," stated Carroll promptly, "but we may hold you for blackmail."

Barker heaved a sigh of relief. "I ain't objectin' to that, Mr. Carroll. It's a small thing when a man has thought he might be strung up."

"Who killed Warren?" questioned the detective.

"Don't you know?" came the surprised answer.

"Yes—but I'm asking you."

"I suppose you're driving at something new," retorted Barker, "but *I* really think Mrs. Lawrence shot him."

"She didn't," answered Carroll. "And there's one thing I want to warn you about right now, Barker. You're the only person except the Chief here, and myself, who knows that Mrs. Lawrence is connected with the case. I want her name kept out of it. Of course that makes it impossible to arrest you for blackmail—and so, if you tell me the entire truth, I'm going to *let* you go free. But if I ever hear of her name in connection with this case I'll know that you have leaked—and I'll get you if it takes me ten years. Understand?"

"Yes, sir, I do—thankin' you, sir. I know which side my bread is buttered on."

"Good. Now I'm telling you that Mrs. Lawrence did *not* shoot Warren. Who did?"

"I don't know—" Suddenly his expression changed. "If it wasn't her, Mr. Carroll—it must have been Mr. Gresham."

"Aa-a-ah! What makes you think that?"

Barker's eyes narrowed. "You give me your word of honor, Mr. Carroll, I ain't goin' to be pinched for blackmail?"

"Yes."

"Well, it was this way, sir. Bein' Mr. Warren's valet I knew he was plannin' to run off with Mrs. Lawrence. I knew that was going to raise an awful row in town—and I knew that Mr. Gresham would do a heap to keep his sister from bein' unhappy as she was going to be if Mr. Warren done as he was plannin'. So I called up Mr. Gresham that night and told him everything but the woman's name. My idea was that he'd bust up the elopement. I went to the station to make sure that Mrs. Lawrence got there—knowin' that once she' was there, if young Mr. Gresham busted things up, I'd be able to blackmail Mrs. Lawrence—her bein' a rich woman. I'm comin' clean with you, Mr. Carroll—"

"Go ahead!"

"I never seen Mr. Gresham at all at the station. And when I seen Mrs. Lawrence get into the taxi and found out the next morning that Mr. Warren's body was found there–of course I couldn't help thinkin' like I did, could I?"

"I suppose not. You're a skunk, Barker–and I hate to let you go. But if the Chief is willing I'm going to do it– because your hide isn't worth Mrs. Lawrence's good name. Now get out!"

"I'm free?" questioned the man eagerly.

"How about it, Leverage?"

"Sure," growled Leverage. "You're the boss, David."

Immediately as Barker left the room Carroll turned to the telephone and called a number.

"Who's that?" questioned Leverage.

"Mrs. Lawrence," answered Carroll. "I want to tell her that she is safe."

Leverage smiled broadly. And as he watched Carroll's eager face he saw an expression of consternation cross it. Carroll covered the transmitter with his hand–

"Good Lord!" he groaned, "it's Evelyn Rogers!"

Leverage chuckled–then listened shamelessly to Carroll's end of the conversation–

"Yes–yes, this is David Carroll–I'm glad you think it was sweet of me to telephone–I want to speak to your sister–She isn't there?–Well, ask her to telephone me at headquarters as soon as she comes in, will you?–Uh-huh!–the Warren case has ended–and that's what I wanted to tell her–I only did my best–Yes–Oh! Say–"

The receiver clicked on the hook. Carroll was grinning as he turned back to his friend–

"Guess what that young thing said when I told her I had solved the Warren case?"

"Tell me, David–I'm a poor guesser."

"She said," returned Carroll gravely–"that I am just the cutest man she has ever known!"

THE END

Other Resurrected Press Mysteries

From the pen of R. Austin Freeman

Dr. John Thorndyke - Lecturer on Medical Jurisprudence and Forensic Medicine. Before Bones, before CSI, before Quincy, M.E – there was Dr. John Thorndyke solving the most baffling cases of Edwardian London using the latest tools of medical science. Read about his cases in:

The Eye of Osiris
John Bellingham, noted Egyptologist has vanished not once but twice in the same day. Now Dr, Thorndyke must unravel the tangled claims on his estate, solve the riddle of the missing man and find the "Eye of Osiris".

The Mystery of 31 New Inn
When Dr. Jervis is whisked away in a coach with no windows to an unknown location to treat a man in a coma from undivulged causes it is Dr. Thorndyke who must come up with the solution.

The Red Thumb Mark
The first of Dr. Thorndyke's cases finds him trying to prove the innocence of a young man accused of being a diamond thief despite the fact that his finger print was found at the scene of the crime.

John Thorndyke's Cases
More cases of medical mysteries as told by his trusted assistant Jervis, M.D. Eight stories of crime and deduction in Edwardian London.

Visit www.resurrectedpress.com

Other Resurrected Press Mysteries

Mysteries on a Train

Before the Orient Express there was:

The Rome Express by Arthur Griffiths
A man is found dead in his first class sleeping compartment on the express from Rome to Paris. Who was his murderer? The Countess? The English General? His brother the clergy man? The maid who has disappeared? Is the French justice system up to solving the crime? Read about it in The Rome Express.

The Passenger from Calais by Arthur Griffiths
Colonel Basil Annesley finds he is the only passenger on the train from Calais to Lucerne. That is until a mysterious woman shows up at the last minute to book a compartment. Who is after her? What is her secret? Is she a criminal or a victim? Read about it in The Passenger from Calais

Visit us at www.resurrectedpress.com

The Fictional Detective
by Greg Fowlkes

Who killed Ezekial O. Handler?

A beautiful dame, a hard-boiled private eye – and a dead body.

It started like any other case. When a famous writer dies in a mysterious car crash, private detective Frank Slade is called in to find answers, but all he finds is more questions. Who killed Ezekial Handler? Who is Janet Nielsen and why is she so interested in finding out? Who is leaving the neatly typed clues? And as Slade tries to find answers to these questions he starts to wonder if the ultimate answer will threaten his very existence.

Read about it in
The Fictional Detective

Visit www.thefictionaldetective.com

About Resurrected Press

A division of Intrepid Ink, LLC, Resurrected Press is dedicated to bringing high quality, vintage books back into publication. See our entire catalogue and find out more at www.ResurrectedPress.com.

About Intrepid Ink, LLC

Intrepid Ink, LLC provides full publishing services to authors of fiction and non-fiction books, eBooks and websites. From editing to formatting, from publishing to marketing, Intrepid Ink gets your creative works into the hands of the people who want to read them. Find out more at www.IntrepidInk.com.

www.ingramcontent.com/pod-product-compliance
Lightning Source LLC
Chambersburg PA
CBHW061156170626
46809CB00003B/1123